George Dixon, Watson

A Descriptive Manual of British Land and Fresh-Water Shells

SALZWASSER VERLAG

George Dixon, Watson

A Descriptive Manual of British Land and Fresh-Water Shells

Reprint of the original, first published in 1859.

1st Edition 2022 | ISBN: 978-3-37512-665-0

Verlag (Publisher): Salzwasser Verlag GmbH, Zeilweg 44, 60439 Frankfurt, Deutschland
Vertretungsberechtigt (Authorized to represent): E. Roepke, Zeilweg 44, 60439 Frankfurt, Deutschland
Druck (Print): Books on Demand GmbH, In de Tarpen 42, 22848 Norderstedt, Deutschland

A

DESCRIPTIVE MANUAL

OF

BRITISH LAND

AND

FRESH-WATER SHELLS,

CONTAINING

DESCRIPTIONS AND FIGURES OF ALL THE SPECIES,

BY DIXON AND WATSON.

PRINTED FOR DIXON AND WATSON, AYTON SCHOOL, NEAR STOKESLEY.

DARLINGTON:
HARRISON PENNEY, PRINTER, PREBEND ROW.

1858.

Pl. VIII.

PREFACE.

It is to be regretted that the study of one of the most pleasing, and, at the same time, most accessible natural history pursuits—the Land and Fresh-water Mollusks of our island—is so much neglected. True, it is, that they are surpassed, both in size and beauty of colouring, by their brethren of the ocean, and for that reason, perhaps, have been overlooked by many; yet there are among these little gems of nature, such beautiful forms, and delicate conformations, that they soon arrest the attention and interest of those, who once commence either to collect or study them.

We believe this branch of natural history will, some day, become much more popular than it is at present. It has many claims upon those who are desirous of becoming acquainted with the varied forms of created life, which nature presents to our view. Perhaps the foremost of these claims, is the fact, that wherever we go, whether it be in the most luxuriant woods, or upon the bleak hills; we have but to look around us, among the herbage, in the waters, or even under the stones which lie at our feet, and some one or other, in all probability several, of these little creatures may be found. In one wood, within the compass of a few square yards, as many as twenty different species have been found.

To the young it especially recommends itself, on account of the limited number of species which our island produces, thus enabling any one, with a little interchange, to form almost a complete collection, in a small compass; and offering a good stepping-stone to the study of nature in its more extended forms, and complicated relations. Having had our lot cast in a district in which the Land and Fresh-water shells abound, perhaps more plentifully than in any other part of the kingdom; and having noticed the never failing source of pleasure, the collecting, examining, naming, and arranging of them has yielded to young persons under our care, we have often urged the principals of other schools to introduce the study among their pupils; knowing well, that when once an acquaintance is formed with them, such is their simple elegance, that they constantly improve in appearance as the acquaintance becomes more intimate, and it will be found, that few who have once begun will be inclined to give up, till the whole subject has been mastered.

But here a difficulty has arisen, a difficulty which we hope, in some degree, the present little volume will remedy; all works on natural history are expensive, and even the simplest complete works on Land and Fresh-water Shells, do not form an exception to the rule. This has induced many to stumble at the threshold of the science. That one volume in a school may enable most of the elder boys to name what they have collected, we admit; but these mostly give up the study, when they return to their respective homes, for want of a *descriptive manual*, and such as do persevere, have to trouble their friends to name any species they may not have previously met with.

These considerations, and the earnest request of many of our valued friends and correspondents, in various parts of the kingdom, have induced us to undertake the present work; which will be found to contain complete descriptions of all the species, and other matter of a suggestive and practical nature, which the experience of several years has enabled us to furnish.

North of England Agricultural School,
Great Ayton.

INTRODUCTION.

THOUGH we do not wish to add to the bulk of the present little volume, we think a few explanatory remarks needful to enable the young chonchologist, to proceed easily in the pursuit of these interesting objects of study.

We have followed the nomenclature adopted by Prof. E. Forbes and S. Hanley, in their magnificent work "British Mollusca," the names there used being those under which the species were first specifically described. Those who are acquainted with this valuable work, will find in many places, we have adopted the same observations, though somewhat condensed, particularly as regards the external form and structure of the animals, some of which we have not had the opportunity of observing. On disputed points we have generally taken the opinion of the most noted conchologists, without entering into detail; but, whenever practicable, and that has been almost always the case, before adopting the remark of any author, we have taken care that the same has been confirmed by our own observations.

With the expectation of this little compilation falling principally into the hands of young persons, or those just commencing the study of conchology in this limited department, we have tried to adjust our remarks to such; we have been particularly careful to point out species that could possibly be confused, noting their characteristic points in contradistinction to those of their nearest allies; we have also generally given not only the locality, but also the circumstances under which each may be found, together with other matter which the experience of several years of collecting, has enabled us to furnish. To the many localities we have gathered from various works, we have added a number which now appear for the first time in print, these, we hope, will prove a valuable addition.

It will be noticed that most of our British species are widely distributed; in almost any district, a radius of a few miles, will supply about three-fourths of the whole number; so that any one, without assistance or exchange, can possess himself of a tolerably large collection. A few, however, seem confined to the Southern and Midland Counties, while one or two are seldom found except in the North: among the former are—*Assiminia Grayana, Testacella haliotoidea, Helix aperta, Helix pomatia, Helix pisana, Helix Carthusiana, Helix obvoluta, Helix revelata, Bulimus acutus, Bulimus Lachamensis, Clausilia biplicata, and Succinea oblonga;* among the latter are *Zonites excavatus, Zonites purus, Helix hybrida, Helix sericea, Helix fusca, Helix limbata, Clausilia dubia, Pupa Anglica, Limnœus Burnetti, Planorbis nautileus, and Acme lineata.* There can be little doubt that Geological formation plays an important part in the distribution of land shells, and for this reason, probably, the southern part of our island produces many species which are seldom, some never, found further north. This is principally owing to the calcareous nature of the rocks. *Helix aperta* and *Testacella haliotoidia* have been found only in the Channel Islands, and would, on that account, be erased from the British fanna, by some naturalists.

The implements required for carrying on the study are few, simple, and not expensive. A SPOON, for scooping-up the water varieties from amongst aquatic plants, which can be made of tin, with fine gauze wire or perforated zinc at the bottom, the gauze must be so fine that it will not allow the smaller *Pisidia, &c.* to pass through; to this a handle five or six feet in length may be attached, or it is often convenient to have it to fix on the end of a walking stick. BOXES, of various sizes, to keep the finer varieties from being broken, and to separate those found in different localities. With these and a small POCKET MICROSCOPE, the conchologist may consider himself fully equipped.

After having collected a considerable number of shells, our first care is to kill the mollusks which inhabit them; this is most speedily and effectually accomplished by pouring boiling water upon them; we then disengage them by means of a needle, fastened to a small handle, or perhaps occasionally use a crooked pin. The very small ones need no cleaning. Our next care should be to have them properly mounted: this of course must depend almost entirely on the taste of the collector. We have found a mahogany box or case, eighteen inches square, and two inches in depth, so made that the top and bottom are of equal depth, the best suited for displaying the whole collection at one view. The shells are attached by gum or glue to the top as well as the bottom of the case. After the inside has been papered out, the names, neatly cut from a printed catalogue, should be arranged in columns, taking care to have sufficient room for the shells, and thus, by a little contrivance, the names of the whole of the species may be made exactly to fill the case. Above the names several specimens of as many kinds as you are possessed of should be fastened; the remainder can be added from time to time, as you are able to meet with them. Boys will find this an excellent plan. For cabinets they are, perhaps, best mounted on separate pieces of wood, with the labels, synonyms, locality, &c. attached. There is an advantage in this latter plan, the specimens can be lifted so as to be more closely examined or even placed under a microscope. Some prefer keeping them in small pill boxes, with the label outside, this plan, too, has its advantages.

We would advise those who are collecting, to obtain more individuals of any species than they want, especially of those that are somewhat rare and local; that so they may have the means of exchanging for others, which they may be in want of.

We have not thought it worth while to burden our pages, with even giving the names of species which have been erroneously introduced into the British Fanna, with the exception of one or two which have found their way into almost every collection, and some which are almost acclimatized. *H. aperta*, which appears in all works on British Conchology, is retained, though not strictly British. One or two shells which are now and then found amongst the debris of rocks or in superficial deposits may be considered as subfossil. In this state we have found, among others, *Succinea oblonga*, *Zua lubrica*, *Bithinia tentaculata*,

Valvata piscinalis, Achatina acicula, Pupa Venetzii. The species found in the older series differ from the recent British Land and Fresh-water Mollusks in being considerably larger, and are more nearly allied to our present tropical species. Had our limits allowed of it, we should have somewhat enlarged our observations on Geological distribution, a branch which has hitherto been overlooked. It would be advisable for readers in different parts of the country, to record in some of our Natural History publications, not only lists of shells found in the district in which they live, but also the circumstances under which they are found, the formation of the rock, or the nature of the water, &c.

We append a few of the many works that can be consulted, by those who are desirous of further information respecting the structure, organization, &c. of these little creatures, than the object of the present work will allow. At the same time we would advise our younger readers to make their own observations and compare them with those of others, rather than learn from works of art what can only be properly acquired by an inspection of nature herself. What could afford more delight than to make the Freshwater varieties the inmates of vivariums, where their peculiarities could be watched day by day, or to colonize our neighbouring woods and hedgerows with some of the land species!

In the wonderful structure and development, as well as the habits of mollusks, there are many peculiarities that are common to all, so that to the reflecting student a thorough investigation of a few of the commoner species, may furnish him with a vast amount of information.

A History of British Mollusca and their Shells; Professor Edward Forbes and Silvanus Hanley.

A Manual of Land and Fresh-Water Shells of the British Islands; William Turton, revised and much enlarged by John Edward Grey.

Illustrations of British Conchology; Thomas Brown.

Testacea Britannica; George Montague.

Historia Vermium Terrestrium et Fluviatilium; O. F. Muller.

Catalogue des Mollusque Terrestris et Fluviatills du pas de Calais; Bouchard Chantreux.

BRITISH LAND AND FRESH WATER SHELLS.

Naturalists have divided all living, sentient beings, into four sub-kingdoms, according to the different types upon which they are constructed, viz.,

SUB-KINGDOM.—I. VERTEBRATA—backboned animals.
" II. MOLLUSCA—soft or pulpy animals.
" III. ARTICULATA—jointed animals.
" IV. RADIATA—rayed, or branched animals.

The animals under consideration in the present volume, belong to Mollusca, the second sub-kingdom, which is divided into the following six classes:—

CLASS I. CEPHALOPODA—head-footed, as cuttle fish.
" II. GASTEROPODA—stomach-footed, as common snail.
" III. PTEROPODA—wing, or fin-footed, as hyalæa.
" IV. BRACHIOPODA—arm-footed, as terebratula.
" V. CONCHIFERA—shell-bearers, as all bivalves.
" VI. TUNICATA—membrane-covered, porophora.

The two classes, Gasteropoda and Conchifera, embrace all the land and fluviatile species.

Commencing at the foot of the scale, the *bivalve* shells will come first under notice.

CLASS V.—CONCHIFERA.

SECTION I.—ACEPHALA LAMELLIBRANCHIATA.

So called from the animal having no head, and its breathing apparatus being expanded into laminæ. The mouth is situated between the four leaflets of the branchia, with a central foot more or less distinct, and compressed, covered by two pair of leaf-like gills, and large leaf-like mantle. The respiratory organs, though within the mantle, are free from it. The two valves of the shell, which protect the animal, are moulded on, and secreted by, the mantle. These valves are united at the back by a ligament, which causes them to expand, and they are drawn together by an adductor muscle attached to the inner surface of each shell. So simple is the construction of the animals that the dissection of a few individuals will convey more knowledge than a volume of explanation.

In this section, only three tribes inhabit the fresh waters of this country.

Tribe I.—Cycladidæ.

Animal—*With front part of the mantle open and plain at the edge; tube of the siphon produced, and either partially separated from their unfringed extremities, or completely united to them. Foot large, and tongue-shaped.*

Shell—*Thin, rather swelling, nearly equal, striated and furrowed, covered by an epidermis, ligament outside, hinge with lateral and cardinal teeth. All the British species are ovoviviparous. This tribe is divided into two genera* —Cyclas *and* Pisidium.

Tribe II.—Unionidæ.

Animal—*With margins of mantle incapable of being reflexed, freely open almost the entire length; a difference in the structure of their hinder borders alone indicates the siphon-tubes; short cirrhi in the branchial region; foot large, broad, compressed.*

Shell—*Equivalve: covered with an epidermis; hinge with or without teeth; ligament external. It includes two genera* —Unio *and* Anodonta.

Tribe III.—Mytilidæ.

Animal—*With edges of mantle united all round except three apertures, one below for the passage of a short strap-shaped foot, with a byssus at the base, and a distinct byssal groove, and two behind; the upper one a hole only, and the lower one produced into a siphon; mouth large and reflexed.*

Shell—*Almost triangular; regular; inequilateral; hinge devoid of teeth; ligament linear, internal. It includes only one genus*—Dreissena.

The *Univalves* come next under notice.

CLASS II.—GASTEROPODA.

SECTION I.—GASTEROPODA PROSOBRANCHIATA.

So called from the animal moving on its stomach and having its organs of breathing in advance of the head. The mouth is usually at the end of a short proboscis, with two tentacles; eyes either placed at the hinder edge of the tentacles, on a separate pedicel, or sessile, at their base; branchia pectinated, or plume-like, in the form of one or more extended filaments, through which they respire the air of the water; the mantle in which the excretory orifices are placed, is entire, and without syphon, forming a receptacle for the breathing organs in the shape of a vaulted chamber over the head; abdomen well developed: sexes distinct. The shell, protecting partly the gills, and partly the other parts of the body, is spiral, with the mouth either entirely round, or half-moon shaped, covered when the animal has retired within its shell, with a horny operculum variously shaped.

In this section there are three tribes found in our fresh waters.

TRIBE I.—NERITIDÆ.

Animal—*With mouth semiovate; tentaculæ slender, awl-shaped; eyes on prominent pedicels, at the hinder edge of the tentacles: foot rather short, oblong, triangular; tongue complicated in its structure, and denticulated; sides of the body simple.*

Shell—*Thick, semi-globose, imperforate; spire with a few whorls only, last whorl very large and expanded; outer lip acute; columella flattened; surface covered with an epidermis; the operculum, which is spiral and has a tooth at the lower edge, just fits the semi-ovate mouth of the shell to which it is attached by two internal processes, forming a hinge on the inner lip, making this genus the connecting link between the univalve aud bivalve shells. It contains only one genus*—Neritina.

Tribe II.—Paludinidæ.

Animal—*With a lengthened broad ovate mouth; head bearing two tentaculæ, which are long, slender, and setaceous at their tips; at the outside of their base, the pedicels on which the eyes are placed subtend; gills single, enclosed; tongue very short with a series of transverse denticles; foot triangularly oblong, bearing on a rounded lobe the operculum. Bisexual. Male organ in the right tentacle, causing these tentacles to be of unequal length in the males.*

Shell—*Conical or turbinated, with a produced spire, covered with a coloured epidermis; mouth ovate or nearly round; peristome thin, entire; operculum corneous, with a nucleus at the centre expanding in concentric rings. This tribe contains three genera*—Paludina, Bithinia, *and* Valvata.

Tribe III.—Littorinidæ.

Animal—*With elongated trunk; head muzzle-shaped, bearing two rather short subulate tentaculæ; the eyes sessile on the outerside of their bases; no lobes on neck; the lobe of the operculum without filamentary process; tongue with dissimilar lateral elements armed with incurved teeth; foot rounded at both ends.*

Shell—*Solid, turbinate, spire produced; mouth ovate not continued; lip of columella appressed; outer lip with sharp edge; operculum corneous, fitting the mouth of the shell, formed spirally by a few rapidly increasing whorls. It includes one genus*—Assiminia.

Section II.—Gasteropoda Pulmonifera.

So called from their moving on their stomachs, and bearing lungs enabling them to breathe the atmosphere. It embraces all the terrestrial mollusca, and the majority of the gasteropods inhabiting fresh water. They are furnished with pulmonary vessels distributed over the walls of a sack or cavity, situated at the back of the neck. The air admitted into this cavity oxygenizes the blood. Those that inhabit the waters have to come periodically to the surface for the purpose of respiration. They have distinct heads, and are furnished with tentaculæ and eyes. They move by the contraction of the disks of their body.

The shells, when present, are mostly spiral or discoid, sometimes patelliform. They are mostly external. In the few instances in which they are internal, they are imbedded in the mantle, and shaped like the finger nail. They are hermaphrodite, and produce their young by eggs, in which the embryos are observed partially clothed with cilia, the movements of which are obvious.

In this section we have six tribes.

Tribe I.—Limacidæ.

Animal—*The well-known land slug. Body semi-cylindrical, soft and fleshy, secreting abundant mucus through the pores of the skin; the breathing cavity covered by a cloak or disk, in the right margin of which the respiratory orifice, and the vent are observable; the head retractile with four retractile tentacles, the upper two provided with eyes; mouth furnished with teeth, with single and long projecting tops.*

Shell—*Either wanting or embedded in the cloak or disk which covers the front part of the body. They feed either at twilight or during the night. It includes three genera* —Arion, Geomalacus *and* Limax.

Tribe II.—Testacellidæ.

Animal—*With elongated body, semi-cylindrical, tapering in front; disk covering and combined with the upper surface of the body, bearing an external shell at the hinder part of the back; head with four tentaculæ, the upper two bearing the eyes, breathing orifice under the right side of the shell, the vent near to it; reproductive orifice behind the upper tentacle on the right side.*

Shell—*External, earshaped, compressed, with a very short spire; mouth very large with a thin outer lip slightly notched at the hinder part. It contains* one genus—Testacellus.

Tribe III.—Helicidæ.

Animal—*Head well developed, with four cylindrical retractile tentaculæ, the upper ones always prominent, bearing on their summits the eyes; end of the tail tapering, without a gland; cavity of the lungs in the anterior part of the body, at the under part of the edge of which is the breathing hole; at the outer base of the right tentacle is the orifice of the generative organs. Motion produced by the successive expansions and contractions of the muscular foot.*

Shell—*Spiral, often turreted, rarely depressed or expanded, never operculated, but this deficiency is made up by the animal, just before hibernating, closing the orifice with a membraneous epiphragm, which will always be found perforated for the admission of air This is by far the largest tribe, including eleven genera*—Vitrina, Zonites, Helix, Bulimus, Pupa, Balæa, Clausilia, Zua, Azeca, Achatina, Succinea.

Tribe IV.—Limnæadæ.

Animal—*With a conical spiral body; an elongated foot; short muzzle with dilated lips, and two compressed tentacles of considerable size, with the eyes placed near their outer base. The tongue is armed with numerous toothed denticles. No operculum.*

Shell—*Variously shaped, spiral, turreted, dextral or sinistral, discoid and even patelliform. Pale, uniform coloured, and clothed with a hard olive or brownish periostraca. It includes four genera*—Physa, Planorbis, Limnæus, *and* Ancylus.

Tribe V.—Auriculidæ.

Animal—*With a broad and ringed muzzle, on which are two subtriangular and cylindrical tentaculæ, with eyes near the inner bases. They have numerous hooked teeth, similar to the Limnæadæ. Foot nearly ovate, without operculum.*

Shell—*Spiral ovate, with denticulated apertures. The septa between the whorls of the shell at the extremity of the body are imperfect. It includes two genera*—Conovulus *and* Carychium.

Tribe VI.—Cyclostomidiæ.

Animal—*With a spiral body; two tentaculæ with eyes at their inner bases; foot ovate. Terrestrial.*

Shell—*Ovate and turreted, strong; mouth oval; operculum consisting of several whorls. It includes, according to the present arrangement, two genera*—Cyclostoma *and* Acme.

CYCLADIDÆ.

Cyclas. *Brugiere.*

Shell—*Subglobose, equivalved, more or less finely striated; cardinal teeth small, sometimes undistinguishable, one in the right and two in the left valve. Lateral teeth developed transversely, distinguished from the Pisidia by being larger, rounder, and more equilateral.*

Animal—*Mantle produced behind forming a siphon, which is divided into two nearly equal tubes.*

C. rivicola. *Leach.* Pl. I, fig. 2.

Shell subglobose, striated concentrically; umbones obtuse; cardinal ligaments distinct.

Tellina cornea; *var. B. Linn.* Cyclas corneà, *Drap.*

This is the largest of British Cycladidæ. Its form is roundish, oval, and very slightly inequilateral. It is comparatively strong and opaque. The valves are covered more or less closely with concentric striæ, which are less distinct on the umbones. The epidermis is glossy and of a brownish green, with darker zones; the umbones have generally a yellow tinge. Interior of a bluish white colour.

Ordinary length five-sixths of an inch, and breadth two-thirds of an inch.

The tubes of the animal slightly tinged with brown, foot and mantle white.

Hab. The river Thames in considerable abundance; it has also been found in the Trent, New River, Lea,

Isis, Cherwell, Mersey, Foss, and other streams in Yorkshire, &c.

C. CORNEA. *Linnæus.* Pl. I, fig. 3 and Pl. VIII, fig. 8.

Shell subglobose, slightly striated concentrically; umbones obtuse; ligaments indistinct.

Tellina cornea, *Linn, Penn.* Cylas rivalis, *Drap.* Tellina rivalis, *Mull.* Cardium corneum, *Pult., &c.*

The shell of this widely-distributed Cyclas is rather thin, and very finely striated. The valves are much swollen in specimens that are fully formed, and of a fawn colour; younger ones a dirty yellow. Length half an inch, and breadth five-twelfths. Tubes of the animal slightly tinged with flesh colour, foot and mantle white.

Hab. Abundant in almost every district, inhabiting slowly-running streams and sometimes stagnant ponds.

C. CALICULATA. *Draparnaud.* Pl. I, fig. 4.

Shell rather rhombic, umbones prominent, capped.

Cyclas lacustris, *Turt, Gray, &c.* Tellina lacustris, *Linn.* Cardium lacustris, *Mont.*

The prominent umbones and extremely fragile character of this species, will readily distinguish it from its congeners. The surface is glassy, of a greyish ash colour, and the valves much more compressed than in *C. cornea.* We have found specimens of this shell one third of an inch long and five-twelfths broad, but they are commonly rather smaller.

Hab. It is by no means an abundant species, but seems to be more plentiful in the north than the south of England. It inhabits stagnant pools and ditches.

C. LACUSTRIS. *Draparnaud.* Pl. I, fig. 5.

"Shell subrhombic, elongate, ovate, thin, inequilateral, and rather compressed, especially below, where the valves meet each other at an acute angle; a little swollen behind the umbones."

A large individual measured five lines in length, and seven in breadth. The general appearance of the species is that of a greatly produced *caliculata,* but devoid of the characteristic beaks.

Hab. Specimens of this shell from which the above description has been taken, are in the valuable collection of Mr. Jeffreys, marked 'Exmouth, 1831, and Dr. Turton's Cabinet,' which seem to be the only specimens ever found in Britain*

Pisidium. *Pfeiffer.*

Shell—*Suboval, equivalve, inequilateral, more or less concentrically striated. Hinge and lateral teeth similar to Cyclas.*

Animal—*Mantle produced behind into a single undivided tube. Foot tongue-shaped and very extensile.*

P. obtusale. *Pfeiffer.* Pl. I, fig. 6.

Shell globose, finely striated, with blunt projecting umbones.

This is the smallest of British *Pisidia,* seldom exceeding one ninth of an inch in length. The depth is equal to the breadth, both being somewhat less than the length. It may be distinguished by its swollen valves, which give it a roundish oval shape. Umbones nearly central. It is generally covered with a rough epidermis of a greenish black colour, margined by a yellowish zone, which, when removed, presents a glossy pale yellow surface.

Hab. It occurs not unfrequently in Cambridgeshire and Oxfordshire, inhabiting small splash pools, and other stagnant waters, and though not common in Scotland or Ireland, several localities in both countries have been recorded.

P. pusillum. *Turton.* Pl. I, fig. 7.

Shell orbicular, oval, scarcely inequilateral, slightly striated; umbones broad and but slightly prominent

Cyclas fontinalis, *Drap, &c.* Cyclas pulsilla, *Turt.*

This species approaches nearest in form to *P. obtusale,* the umbones being nearly central; but it is more compressed and less glossy, when the epidermis, common to most of the species, has been removed. Its colour is generally a tawny white. It sometimes attains a seventh of an inch in length and an eighth in breadth.

* Forbes and Hanley's "British Mollusca," Vol. II, pp. 118, 119.

Hab. It is very generally distributed, inhabiting stagnant pools, frequently in great abundance.

P. CINEREUM. *Alder.* Pl. I, fig, 8.

Shell broadly ovate, greyish, rather compressed, finely striated with one or two evident sulcations which form darker zones across the shell; umbones obtuse, and slightly produced.

The peculiar milky ash colour and dark zones, together with the compressed shape of this shell, readily distinguish it from the other *Pisidia,* independently of its being much larger (*P. amnicum* excepted.) We have found specimens about a quarter of an inch long, and one fifth broad, in a running stream in the neighbourhood of Guisbro' in Cleveland, though it is generally rather less.

Hab. It is by no means so common as some of the other species. Stagnant or still pools it most frequently inhabits, though sometimes found in running streams and even rivers. Scabro', near Newcastle, Preston, Croydon Canal, Bath, and Exmouth are recorded localities. It is distributed sparingly over Ireland and Scotland.

P. NITIDUM. *Jenyns.* Pl. I, fig. 9.

Shell orbiculate, very shining, oval, with fine striæ, more deeply marked on the umbones.

The animal, according to Jenyns, is white; siphon short and funnel shaped, with a patulous aperture, the margin of which is more or less crenated or plicated. The shell of this species is difficult to distinguish from *P. pusillum,* except by the deeper striæ upon the umbones (which require a searching examination), and its lustrous appearance, being seldom coated with mud. The larger specimens are an eighth of an inch in length, and nearly as broad. Jenyns first described this shell in the Trans. of Cambridge Phil. Soc., from specimens obtained in the ditches in Battersea Fields and other parts of Surrey, where, he says "it is widely distributed but seldom abundant."

Hab. Streams of clear water, Surrey. It has also been found near Scarbro', in Northumberland, near

Darlington, and North Stainley, near Ripon, &c. It is generally distributed in Ireland, and several localities are recorded in Scotland.

P. PULCHELLUM. *Jenyns.* Pl. I, fig. 10.

Shell obliquely ovate, deeply striate, inequilateral; umbones simple, rather blunt.

Pisidium fontinale, *Brown.* Cyclas fontinalis, *Brown.*

This species varies very much both in shape and size, sometimes being smaller than *P. obtusale*, and sometimes almost as large as *P. cinereum;* but it may generally be known by its deeper striæ, more shining appearance, and by being more inequilateral than the others which have been described. On account of the multiplicity of shapes which this shell assumes, many varieties have been appended to the species, by most conchologists, all of which seem more or less to diverge into one another. Its colour varies from an ashy hue to a yellowish white.

Hab. It is one of the commonest of the smaller *Pisidia*, being distributed generally over England, Ireland, and Scotland; inhabiting both running streams and stagnant pools.

P. HENSLOWIANUM. *Sheppard.* Pl. I, fig. 11.

Obliquely oval, finely striated, ventricose; umbones acute, with a laminar projection.

With the exception of the laminar projection and its greater ventricoseness, the description of *P. pulchellum* would equally apply to this species. The surface is generally rather glossy, of an ashy grey or yellowish horn colour. The length varies from a sixth of an inch to two lines and a half.

Hab. Ditches and slowly flowing streams; the recorded localities are few. River Cam, Thames at Henley, Ackworth, and several places near Oxford.*

* James Dalton, B.A., who has kindly furnished us with many localities, states "it has become abundant since the introduction of the American ANACHARIS ALSINASTRUM. Formerly the shell was very rare."

P. AMNICUM. *Muller.* Pl. I, fig. 12.

Ovate; very inequilateral, deeply sulcated, striated; umbones, somewhat blunt.

Tellina amnica, *Mull, Turt, &c.* Cylas amnicum, *Turt.*

This species is more inequilateral than any other *Pisidium,* and considerably larger in size. These characteristics, together with the deep sulcations and striæ, will readily distinguish it from its congeners. The valves are moderately ventricose in adult, though much compressed in young specimens. It is comparatively strong; and though generally semi-transparent, it is frequently scarcely diaphanous. Of an olivaceous ash colour, with a broad marginal zone of a yellow tint.

Specimens may sometimes be found nearly half an inch in length, and a third in breadth.

Hab. An abundant species; delighting more especially in running streams, though by no means confined to them.

UNIONIDÆ.

Unio. *Retzius.*

Shell—*Equivalve, inequilateral; hinge, with two teeth in each valve, the one short, irregular, and sub-striated, the other elongated, compressed, lateral; ligament exterior.*

Animal—*Thick, mantle freely open in front, with simple edges; branchial region fringed with numerous cirrhi. Foot large, broad, compressed.*

U. TUMIDUS. *Retzius.* Pl. III, fig. 2.

Wedge shaped; tumid; umbones prominent; rugose; anterior teeth thick, high, and conical.

Unio Ovalis. *Flem, &c.*

The external appearance, both as regards colour and shape, varies considerably in this shell, still it is not very difficult to distinguish it from the only other recognized British species. It is extremely solid, with large and strong anterior teeth. The valves are unequally ventricose, swelling in front, and compressed behind;

the surface being generally painted more or less distinctly with rays of colour, varying from brown to a bright green or yellow; occasionally they are met with of a uniform brown, or purplish tinge. They vary from two and a half to three inches in length, by about an inch and a half in the broadest part.

Hab. Found abundantly in some of the streams in the south of Lancashire and Yorkshire; it has also been found in the New River, Avon, Kennet, Ouse, &c.

U. PICTORUM. *Linnæus.* Pl. III, fig. 1.

Oval, oblong, posterior end not cuneiform; of a yellowish green colour interspersed with brownish zones; anterior teeth compressed, elevated, crenate.

Mya pictorum. *Linn.* Unio rostrata. *Lam.*

One of the distinguishing peculiarities of this *Unio* is that its dorsal and ventral margins run almost parallel. The rays of colour also generally so conspicuous in *U. tumidus* are wanting here. Internally it is white, or approaching salmon colour. It frequently attains a greater length than *U. tumidus*; breadth about the same.

Hab. The recorded localities are numerous, Kennet, Avon, several of the Yorkshire rivers, Severn, and almost all canals having a muddy bottom; it has not been found further north than Winyard.

U. Batavus, and U. ovalis we have rejected, the former appears to be foreign, and the latter only a distorted form of *U. tumidus.*

U. MARGARITIFERUS. *Linnæus.* Pl. I, fig. 1.

Ovate, oblong, thick, solid; epidermis brownish black; cardinal teeth, thick, conical; no lateral teeth.

Mya margaritifera, *Linn, Retz., &c.* Alasmodon magaritifera, *Gray.*

This is the shell which obtained so much celebrity amongst the ancients on account of the pearls which are sometimes found in the body of the animal. These pearls seem to be malformations, and are generally formed between the two films or skins that line the shell. Their composition is much the same as that of the inner portion of the shell, being nacreous, and possessing a dull lustre. Some naturalists suppose they are caused by particles of sand, or other irritating substances, getting into the stomach, or other organs; and, the animal to remedy the annoyance, surrounds them with a coating of pearl. Others affirm that they are the products of disease, and correspond to the calculi in some animals.

The average length is from four to five inches, and about two in breadth.

Hab. Most frequently found in mountain streams, hence they are abundant in Wales, Cumberland, Lancashire, the north of Yorkshire, and the hilly parts of Cornwall and Devon. The Linn, Eden, and Yorkshire Esk abound with them.

ANADONTA. *Brugiere.*

Shell—*Oblong, equivalve, generally thin in proportion to the size; inequilateral; hinge without teeth, but furnished with a lamina.*

Animal—*Much the same as* Unio.

A. CYGNEA. *Linnæus.* Pl. II, fig. 1.

Perhaps no shell illustrates the change of form and appearance, which the same species exhibits, from being matured under different circumstances as regards climate, geological formation, and the nature of its food, more evidently than the present. By some writers it has been divided into a number of species, whilst others have endeavoured to classify the different forms under several varieties. The former arrangement is, however, quite exploded, while in adopting the latter, we own it offers many difficulties.

The normal form is elongated oval, moderately ventricose, not very solid; the lines of formation at pretty regular distances; posterior end, not beaked, but roundly attenuated.

The colour of the epidermis is olivaceous yellow green.

var. CELLENSIS. *Gray*. Shell larger, more ventricose, thinner, and more brittle; more produced behind, and epidermis of a greener tint.

Hab. Ponds in very still water.

var. VENTRICOSA. *Pfeif*. Valves more solid and swollen; in shape, rhombic oval; the epidermis being often beautifully coloured.

var. ANATINA. *Pfeif*. Smaller than the above; some of the lines of growth so indistinct as to show a considerable breadth smooth and glossy; hinder extremity broad and sub-rhomboidal; dorsal line rising behind so as to give it a winged appearance; epidermis a bright green with rayed lines.

var. ROSTRATA. *Pfeif*. Rather rhombic; much produced behind, so as to form a sort of beak; short and rounded in front; colour generally brownish.

var. AVONENSIS. *Gray*. Very nearly connected with the preceding, but more rounded; ventricose, thick, solid, and slopes rather angularly behind.

Hab. The localities of this species are so numerous that it is less difficult to say where it is not, than where it is found. Though lakes and ponds which have a constant influx of fresh water, but possess, at the same time, an unruffled surface, except when disturbed by winds, seem most favourable to its perfect development, yet running streams with sandy or gravelly bottoms furnish a stunted race of less pleasing appearance. In collecting this species (as in others which vary much), the young conchologist should carefully label his specimens with the locality, adding a few remarks on the nature of the water, the character of the bottom, or any other circumstance which could have any effect upon the shell, or its inmate.

MYTILIDÆ.

DREISSENA. *Van Beneden*.

Shell—*Equivalve, very inequilateral, triangular; characterized by a small transverse plate under* the hinge within.

Animal—*Mantle closed, except a passage for the foot and two syphons; retracting muscular cords united into a single bundle with one point of attachment.*

D. POLYMORPHA. *Pallas.* Pl. III, fig. 3 and 4.

The remarkable rapidity with which this shell has spread in numerous localities on our island, is one of the most interesting facts connected with it, showing how readily species become naturalized when the climate and situation are suitable. Naturalists are undecided how it has got introduced, whether adhering to the bottom of ships it has survived a passage through the salt water of the sea from the mouths of rivers in Sweden, Russia, &c.; or by adhering to the timber exported from those countries, it has remained alive for so long a time out of water.

Hab. Most of our canals which communicate with seaport towns in the midland and northern counties, living in gregarious masses on stones and pieces of timber.

NERITIDÆ.

NERETINA. *Lamark.*

Shell—*Semiglobular; without an umbilicus; generally thick; spire of few whorls, last whorl large; aperture semicircular, furnished with an operculum having a tooth on its lower margin.*

Animal—*Tentacles awl shaped; eyes on short pedicels at the outer side of their base; foot rather short, triangularly oblong.*

N. FLUVIATILIS. *Linnæus.* Pl. IV, fig. 1 and Pl. VIII, fig. 1.

The peculiar markings of this shell, together with its form, will readily distinguish it from any other of our species. The dark ground is variously chequered with spots of yellowish white, brown, purple, or pink, but they are often obscured by an incrustation from the water, which seems to serve as a protection from animals which would otherwise seize them as prey.

About three-eighths of an inch long, and a quarter of an inch broad. Convex or flat above, and slightly incurved underneath.

Hab. Rivers, especially the larger ones, as the Thames, Trent, Ouse (near York), Humber, Severn, and Avon. We have frequently obtained dead specimens from the ballast hills near Middlesbro', which have been brought from the mouths of other rivers.

PALUDINIDÆ.

PALUDINA. *Lamark.*

Shell—*Spiral, convex; mouth nearly round, operculum long, consisting of concentric rings, terminating in a small nucleus on the inner side; epidermis coloured.*

Animal—*With a lengthened muzzle; foot large; tentaculæ two, those of the male unequal. Female ovo-viviparous.*

P. LISTERI. *Forbes and Hanley.* Pl. IV, fig. 5, and Pl. VIII, fig. 3.

Shell thin, spiral; five volutions very distinctly marked; mouth large and open.

Paludina vivipara. *Gray.*

This shell is chiefly found in the midland and southern counties. It may be distinguished from *P. vivipara* by the volutions being more inflated, the shell thinner, the last whorl larger and more open, and the whorls at the apex very distinct, and terminating in a sharp point.

Full grown individuals measure about an inch in length, by three fourths of an inch in breadth.

Hab. Slowly-running rivers and canals. The recorded localities are the rivers Ex, Taw, Lea, Isis (at Blenheim), and a stream near York, &c.

P. VIVIPARA. *Linnæus.* Pl. IV, fig. 6.

Sharper, and more produced than the last. Shell rather thicker and not so translucid; volutions six in number, with brown bands running parallel with the sutures. The colouring paler, the whorls less prominent, and consequently the sutures not so deep; mouth more contracted; apex blunt.

Paludina achatina. *Gray, Lam, &c.*

Length the same as *P. Listeri,* but not quite so broad.

Hab. Abundant in the Cherwell, Oxfordshire, &c.

Bithinia. *Gray.*

Shell—*More or less spiral, covered with a horny epidermis, of a yellow colour; mouth ovate, slightly angular above.*

Animal—*Muzzle lengthened; two tentaculæ with eyes at the extremities, those of the male equal Foot obtuse, with thick shelly operculum. Oviparous.*

B. tentaculata. *Gray.* Pl. IV, fig. 7.

Oval, spiral, with five modertely convex volutions of a yellowish colour, smooth and semitransparent; no umbilicus.

Helix tentaculata, *Linn.* Paludina impura, *Lam., Sowb., &c.*

Medium size, about five-twefths of an inch in length, and one in breadth, though we have met with individual specimens much larger. It is seldom covered with an extraneous epidermis, if covered, it is readily removed, and presents a smooth, shining exterior. The shell is moderately thick. Operculum thick and shelly.

Hab. Common all over England except the extreme north. It is found in ditches, canals, and slowly-running streams.

B. Leachii. *Sheppard.* Pl. IV, fig. 8.

Somewhat resembles the young of B. tentaculata, but is more conical, the whorls are better defined, and it has a small oblique umbilicus.

Bithinia ventricosa, *Gray.* Paludina ventricosa, *Brown.*

Besides the above distinguishing characteristics, the final volution is shorter, more ventricose and nearly circular. Ordinary length a quarter of an inch, and breadth two lines.

Hab. Many localities in the region of the Thames, and the south of England generally; but also met with occasionally in the north. Streams near York and the south of Durham. It is not so plentiful as the preceding species.

Valvata. *Muller.*

Shell—*With a somewhat elevated or a discoid spire; mouth circular; operculum horny, concentrically spiral.*

Animal—*Muzzle produced; cylindrical elongated tentacles, with eyes at the hinder extremities.*

V. PISCINALIS. *Muller.* Pl. IV, fig. 4.

Somewhat globular, with an elevated deeply sutured spire of three whorls, above the last volution; umbilicus a whitish colour.

The two species of *Valvata* differ much in general appearance, the one being comparatively long and spiral, the other discoid and depressed.

Shell nearly a quarter of an inch in length and the same in breadth.

Hab. Canals, streams, and ponds. It is generally distributed all over the British Isles, though by no means common in some districts.

V. CRISTATA. *Muller.* Pl. IV, fig. 3.

Discoid, flat; spire level or somewhat below the last volution.

The whorls are cylindrical, three in number and deeply suturated. The shell is thin and of a light horn colour; about one tenth of an inch in diameter; somewhat resembles a *Planorbis*, but is readily distinguished by the operculum.

Hab. Ditches and ponds in many parts of Britain, and where found they are usually plentiful. Distributed all over Ireland.

LITTORINIDÆ.

ASSIMINIA. *Gray.*

Shell—*Spiral, conical, smooth. Operculum corneous.*

Animal—*Head, muzzle-shaped; two tentacles with eyes at the extremities.*

A. GRAYANA. *Jeffreys.* Pl. IV, fig. 2, and Pl. VIII, fig. 2.

Ovate; of a brown colour; mouth of the animal elliptical.

This shell is never found except in brackish water. The spire which consists of several whorls is rather acute. It is about a quarter of an inch in length.

Hab. The mouths of rivers amongst confervæ, &c.

Found plentifully at Greenwich marshes and other places in the south of England.

LIMACIDÆ.

ARION. *Ferussac.*

Shell—*Oblong, generally of a soft spungy nature, but hardens upon exposure to the atmosphere, situated in the disk covering the anterior part of the body, undeveloped.*

Animal—*Somewhat cylindrical, lanceolate; tentacles four in number, two of which have eyes at their extremities; mantle elliptical.*

A. EMPIRICORUM. *Ferussac.* Pl. V, fig. 1.

Body generally black, and somewhat grooved; shield ovate; shell spongy.

Limax ater, *Linn.* Arion ater, *Gray.*

So abundant, that during wet weather the fields and paths are strewed with them in all directions. They are naturally herbivorous, though at times carnivorous, and so voracious that they do a great amount of injury to the farmer and gardener, who wage an exterminating war with them and others of the mollusca family. It is somewhat variable in colour according to the locality and other natural circumstances; the prevailing hue is a slaty black, but it is occasionally of a reddish brown, and sometimes almost white.*

Hab. Woods, gardens, and moist places all over Britain.

A. FLAVUS. *Muller.* Pl. V, fig. 4.

More elongated than A. empiricorum; disk more oblong; secreting a yellow mucus.

About an inch in length and of a whitish colour, excepting the shield and posterior parts, which are a faint yellow.

* The best way of preserving the land slugs for collections is in spirits of wine. They can be deprived of life almost instantaneously by pouring boiling water over them, which should be done while the animal is stretched out. They should be then placed in a small glass tube, one end of which has been closed, the tube filled with spirits of wine and the other end closed.

Hab. Moist and rocky places. The only recorded locality is at the side of the turnpike road, Westgate Hill.

A. HORTENSIS. *Ferussac.* Pl. V, fig. 3.

Slaty blue colour, streaked, elongated, shell rather concave.

This pretty little slug is common in the north of England, both in woods and gardens, in company with *A. empiricorum.* It is variable both in size and colour, but seldom measures more than an inch and a half in length, and is always streaked along the upper part of the body.

Hab. Moist woods and gardens, where it should be sought for immediately after a shower, in summer weather.

GEOMALACUS. *Allman.*

Shell—*Ovate, in a sheath similar to Arion.*

Animal—*Elongated cylindrical, lanceolate; four tentacles, two of which are furnished with eyes.*

G. MALCULOSUS. *Allman.* Pl. V, fig. 6.

This genus is distinguished by the position of the respiratory orifice, being at the right side of the disk at the anterior margin, the caudal gland, and the position of the reproductive orifice. It is by far the most beautiful of the slug tribe, the body being spotted with bright yellow.

Hab. The south of Ireland, in damp rocky situations. In many places plentiful.

LIMAX. *Linnæus.*

Shell—*Oval, of a white or cream colour, and found embedded in an oblong disk.*

Animal—*Head furnished with four tentacles, two of which have eyes, retractile like the former; tail lanceolate without a mucous gland; spiracle on the hinder margin; pulmonary cavity behind it: orifice of the reproductive system at the hinder side of the right tentacle.*

L. AGRESTIS. *Muller.* Pl. IV, fig. 9.

Of a grey colour, mantle large, ovate and rounded behind; shell small; keel short and always slanting.

The commonest, the most voracious, and consequently the most destructive to almost all kinds of vegetables is this little slug; it is the pest of the flower garden, which seems to be its favourite resort. It is said to produce many families in a year, and has been known to lay as many as two hundred eggs at one time! The mucus is white, which when dry leaves a white streak.

Hab. Almost every garden in the country; also fields, damp lanes, &c.

L. CINEREUS. *Muller.* Pl. IV, fig. 12.

Animal of a cinereous colour, with elongated spots on the back· keel long and straight, somewhat carinated towards the extremity; shield produced behind; shell thin, flat, slightly concave, and pearly white.

Limax maximus, *Gray.*

The largest of the Limaces, sometimes measuring five or six inches in length. It is not so common as the former species, though found plentifully in all parts of the British Isles. The shell is large, generally measuring five or six lines in length and somewhat more than half the breadth. The animal when at rest does not contract its body, like most of the other land slugs, into a semi-spheroid, but simply withdraws its head under the mantle.

Hab. Common everywhere in suitable places. It prefers a shady situation under trees and stones.

L. ARBORUM. *Bouchard Chantereux.* Pl. IV, fig. 14.

Back round, somewhat flatter at the tail; shield peculiarly wrinkled, obtuse in front but pointed behind, of a peculiar tawny grey colour; shell of an oblong shape, rather convex above and concave below.

This snail is usually found under decayed wood, on which it is said to subsist, and hence obtains the name of the tree slug. It resembles *cinereus* in some of its stages, but seldom attains the same size, and may be distinguished from it by the position of the spiracle and the shape of the mantle; it is also more attenuated, the hinder part more lanceolate, and the anterior tentacles much shorter.

Hab. Generally distributed over the British Isles, on trees or near them.

L. FLAVUS. *Linnæus.* Pl. V, fig. 4.

Yellowish brown colour, head and tentacles bluish; mantle large, rounded behind, wrinkled; the extremity of the tail carinated; shell thin.

Limax variegatus, *Drap.*, *&c.*

The cellar slug is a large species about the same size as *L. cinereus*, but differs from it in having a smaller head, smaller tentacles, and being generally of a yellowish grey or fawn colour. The mucus is colourless. The shell is oval, extremely thin, four or five lines in length, and of a pearly white colour.

Hab. Plentiful in almost every damp cellar, and other dark, damp places. The recorded localities are few, but there is no doubt of its being abundant all over England.

L. BRUNNEUS. *Draparnaud.* Pl. V, fig. 2.

Uniform dark brown colour; with a paler mantle, which is wrinkled; neck long; the extremity of the tail carinated.

This slug is similar in size and shape to *agrestis*, being about an inch in length. The mucus is colourless.

Hab. The only recorded localities for this slug are in the north-east of England; we have found many specimens in various parts of Cleveland, Yorkshire, though it is by no means plentiful. It is found in similar situations to the other *Limaces*, taking refuge under stones during the dry weather. It is probably partial to a damp peaty soil.

L. TENELLUS. *Muller.* Pl. IV, fig. 14.

Back rounded, compressed near the tail; shield wrinkled; colour yellow; mucus yellow.

The rarest of British slugs. Only one specimen has been met with, which was discovered in a wood at Allansford, near Shotley Bridge. It does not exceed an inch and a quarter in length. Tentacles black. The shield is rounded behind and covered with fine concentric circles.

L. SOWERBII. *Ferussac.* Pl. IV, fig. 10.

Mantle short, truncated behind; granulated; yellowish brown colour; tentacles bluish black; shell small, oval, and convex beneath; keel obvious.

L. carinatus, *Gray*.

This slug may be distinguished by its prominent keel and short truncated mantle. It is about three inches in length. The shell is two or three lines long.

Hab. Gardens and damp places in the south of England. We have found single specimens in the north of Yorkshire, though by no means common. Many localities in Ireland are recorded.

L. GAGATES. *Draparnaud.* Pl. IV, fig. 11.

Obtuse, back carinated, bluish grey colour, lanceolate.

This rare slug is only recorded as having been found in one place in England, but has been taken in many places in Ireland. The mantle is very obtuse, and in outward appearance much more resembles that of an *Arion* than a *Limax*. The shell is small, oval, and plano-convex. The head is of the same colour as the body, but the tentacles are generally rather darker.

Hab. Shady places under stones, Ireland.

TESTACELLIDÆ.

TESTACELLA. *Cuvier.*

Shell—***Strong and large for the size of the animal, situated at the extremity of the body; external, auriform-shape, with a minute spire.***

Animal—***Elongated; of a yellowish, reddish, or grey hue; tentacles cylindrical, four in number, the two anterior ones being furnished with eyes.***

T. HALIOTOIDEA. *Draparnaud.* Pl. V, fig. 5.

Testacellus haliotoideus, *Gray, &c.*

This species is confined to the south of England, and Ireland, where it has been most probably introduced; it was first found in the Channel Isles. The genus is intermediate between the slug and the snail; the shell and animal being like the former, but differing from it in the position of the shell, which is placed on the posterior part of the body and external. They are carnivorous, and live for the most part in holes under the ground.

Hab. The islands of Guernsey and the other Channel islands, and in or near nursery gardens in the south and south-west of England.

A spurious species, *T. Maugii*, has been introduced by some conchologists, from having been found in a nursery garden near Bristol, and at Devizes.

HELICIDÆ.

VITRINA. *Draparnaud.*

Shell—*Exceedingly thin, subglobular, with a depressed spire of a few whorls; pellucid.*

Animal—*Lanceolate; mantle large, furnished with a lobe on the right side.*

V. PELLUCIDA. *Muller.* Pl. V, fig. 12.

Shell small in proportion to the animal, very thin, diaphanous, colour varying from a white or yellow tint, to that of a beautiful green

Helix pellucida, *Mull.* H. elliptica, *Brown.*

This beautiful little mollusk is a connecting link between the slugs and snails, having the shield-like mantle of the one and the external globular shell of the other. The animal also is only partly retractile. The shell is so thin and brittle that a very slight crush would break it. It is as its name implies vitreous, more so perhaps than any other shell.

Hab. Plentiful in all parts of the country among moss, or buried a few inches under the surface of the ground. May be found among decayed leaves and peat, when not too moist, in great abundance.

ZONITES. *Gray.*

Shell—*Spiral, more or less discoid; spire of many whorls, depressed; mouth nearly circular.*

Animal—*Lanceolate, tentacles four, the posterior ones small; mantle reflexed.*

Z. cellarius. *Muller*. Pl. V, fig. 8.

Shell discoid, opaque white beneath, a yellowish horn colour above, shining and smooth; whorls five or five and a half in number.

Helix cellaria, *Mull.*, *&c.*

There is sometimes a difficulty in distinguishing this species from Z. *alliarius*, when the animal is not present, but there is in the one under notice a peculiarly pellucid milkiness of colouring, which is never present in the succeeding species; the spire also is more flattened, and it attains to a considerably larger size; in fact it is the largest of our *Zonites*, sometimes measuring half an inch in diameter, when found in favourable situations as drains and sewers. They prefer damp places amongst luxuriantly growing weeds. We were once somewhat surprised, when turning over a plot of ground in the early part of the spring, to find a number of these shells, frequently at the depth of eight or ten inches below the surface, where no doubt they had descended to pass the winter in a state of torpor, and the weather had not been sufficiently genial to call them forth into more active life.

Hab. May be found in almost every district very abundantly, at the roots of damp grass, moss, &c.

Z. alliarius. *Miller*. Pl. V, fig. 13.

Shell slightly convex, nearly flat, thin, horn coloured, smooth and shining; four volutions; slightly white underneath and near the umbilicus.

Helix alliaria, *Brown*, *&c.*

Though the family of *Zonites* is somewhat puzzling to beginners, yet we think, by a little close attention, the diligent observer will be able to overcome the difficulties which he may meet with; perhaps the greatest obstruction is the liability to confound the young of the larger, with the full grown smaller ones. *Z. alliarius* when living may always be easily distinguished from the rest, by the strong garlic smell which the animal emits, especially when irritated; this is a remarkable fact and has no parallel amongst the other British Land

and Fresh-water Molluscs; for what purpose it is designed we are quite ignorant, though probably as a means of defence. It approaches nearest to *Z. cellarius* and *nitidulus* in general appearance and form, but from the former it may be known by its small size and darker colour, besides not being so flat in the spire; whilst it is darker than the latter and more lustrous.

Hab. It is universally diffused through the British Isles, in various localities; its most favourite haunts are woods, amongst the grass and moss at the roots of trees, under stones, and logs of fallen timber.

Z. NITIDULUS. *Draparnaud.* Pl. V. fig. 9.

Shell flat, of a dull waxy appearance above, dirty yellowish horn colour, opaque; mouth large.

Helix nitidula, *Alder.*, *&c.*

This is almost sure to be the first *Zonites* with which the young naturalist will form an acquaintance, for there is not a hedge-row, wood, or garden where it may not be met with; almost every locality seems favourable, though like most of the *Zonites* it prefers the damp wood. The only species with which it is likely to be confounded are *cellarius* and *alliarius*, from both it may be distinguished by the absence of that lustre which is a marked feature in their appearance.

The shell is about three tenths of an inch in diameter.

Hab. Exceedingly plentiful, almost every hedgerow will furnish a number of specimens at the roots of grass.

Z. PURUS. *Alder.* Pl. V, fig. 14.

Shell depressed, smooth, transparent white; whorls four; umbilicus large.

Helix nitidula, *Drap.* Helix pura, *Brown*, *Alder*.

This is the most delicate of the *Zonites*, being fragile and generally of a transparent white colour, though there is a variety of a light horn colour, about one eighth of an inch in diameter. The species with which this may be confounded are *radiatulus* and *crystallinus*. It is destitute of the longitudinal markings so apparent and universal in *radiatulus*, whence its name; *radiatulus* is also a stronger shell, and the outer whorl greater in comparison to the size. *Crystallinus* is much smaller and always of a milky white colour throughout, and remarkably thin.

Hab. Hedge-rows and woods are its favourite resorts, generally preferring a moist situation, adhering to the decaying leaves, and lurking amongst the roots of grass and moss.

Z. RADIATULUS. *Alder*. Pl. V, fig. 10.

Shell depressed, horn colour, regularly striated on both disks; whorls four; umbilicus large.

Helix radiatula, *Brown, &c.*

This is one of the most interesting species of the genus, partaking as it does somewhat of the character of a Helix, and seems to be the connecting link between the two. This is more strikingly the case if we pay much regard to the old distinction of a streaked outer lip being characteristic of a Helix in contradistinction to a *Zonites*. If a full grown specimen of this shell be carefully examined, the streakings of the outer lip cannot fail to be perceived, the lip is also of a different colour, being whitish, and is more opaque than the rest of the shell.

The longitudinal ridges and furrows, together with the greater depth and breadth of the outer whorl in comparison with the rest of the shell, will readily distinguish it from the brown variety of *Z. purus*, for which alone it can be mistaken. About one fifth of an inch in diameter.

Hab. We have met with it most abundantly in old grassy fields or commons, where the ground is somewhat damp and favours the growth of mosses, at the roots of which it is generally found.

Z. NITIDUS. *Muller*. Pl. V, fig. 15.

Shell depressed, remarkably shining, brownish horn colour; whorls four and a half or five; umbilicus large.

Helix lucida, *Brown*. Zonites lucidus, *Gray*.

This species is unmistakable when the animal and its shell have not parted company, for the former is quite black, which is not the case with any of the other *Zonites*, being generally of a greyish colour; the shell too is of a deeper hue and much brighter. It is similar to *Z. excavatus*, in having a large umbilicus, but the latter has a number of longitudinal striæ, which are not found in *nitidus*. From what we have collected we should consider them gregarious. About a quarter of an inch in diameter.

Hab. It chiefly inhabits marshy ground where it may sometimes be found in great numbers, on the stems of rushes and other aquatic plants, and on the tufts of sedges which grow on the margin of ponds and streams. It is pretty generally distributed, but somewhat local.

Z. EXCAVATUS. *Bean.* Pl. V, fig. 16.

Shell depressed, small, shining, regularly striated, of a horn colour; umbilicus very capacious; aperture orbicular lunate.

Helix excavata, *Alder, &c.*

In form and appearance this shell comes nearest to *nitidus*, but is of a lighter colour, has a larger umbilicus, and furnished with longitudinal striæ, and not nearly so lustrous.

Hab. This species is the least common of the *Zonites*, perhaps owing to the nature of the habitats which it frequents; these are chiefly the roots of plants in woods, and beneath fallen stems and trunks of trees which have been for some considerable time on the ground. It is always found, as far as we have been able to judge, in districts where the Carboniferous formation is prevalent. We have found it in woods near Wakefield, and have had specimens sent from near Dewsbury and Penketh, all in such districts, and it has been discovered near Newcastle and Scarbrough. It is, we think, an illustration of the fact that Geological formations have much to do with the distribution of animal life, especially in its lower developments, not so much certainly as climate, yet more than has generally been admitted.

Z. crystallinus. *Muller*. Pl. V, fig. 11.

Minute, nearly flat, glossy, a milky white colour, almost transparent; mouth lunate; umbilicus small.

Helix crystallina, *Mull.*

This is the smallest of the British Mollusks at present comprised under the name *Zonites*, and is a sparkling and perfectly transparent little gem. It may be distinguished from all the others by the closeness of the whorls, which are also more numerous than those of *purus*, which it most nearly resembles. The shell is seldom more than an eighth of an inch in diameter.

Hab. Almost every locality furnishes this species. It is found in woods, hedge-rows, and mossy fields, though seldom in very great numbers. Like most of the other species it seems to prefer a damp to a dry situation, and is frequently a little beneath the surface of the earth.

Helix. *Linnæus.*

Shell—*More or less spiral, globose or discoid; outer lip thickened; variously coloured, without an epidermis; mouth lunated.*

Ainmal—*With four tentaculæ, an elongated depressed foot; tail lanceolate; body produced and spiral.*

H. aperta. *Born*. Pl. VI, fig. 1.

Shell subglobose, thin, brownish green colour, somewhat wrinkled; mouth large and wide.

Helix naticoides, *Drap, &c.*

In deference to the authority of Professor Forbes and S. Hanley we retain this Helix as a British species. Only one mutilated specimen has been discovered, and that in the island of Guernsey, no doubt having been brought over from France, in the south of which country they are abundant, and are eaten in Provence as a delicacy. The above specimen is in the British Museum.

Hab. Hedges amongst nettles.

H. ASPERSA. *Muller*. Pl. VI, fig. 2.

Shell subglobose, brown colour with dark coloured bands; whorls four; aperture ovato-lunate.

This most beautiful of British snails is very generally distributed over England, Scotland, and Ireland, and may be found at any time under stones, in holes in old walls, and amongst the hedge-rows. During the winter they collect in great numbers in sheltered nooks, fastening themselves together so as to form a gregarious mass of sometimes scores of individual specimens. The process of hybernation may be best seen in this species on account of its size and great abundance. (See Penny Cyclopædia). There is little fear of confounding this with any other British species, though it varies considerably in form and colour; the prevailing colour is chocolate, though we occasionally meet with specimens almost entirely white. The mouth is white. When irritated the animal emits a peculiar green mucus. Sometimes used as food for pulmonary affections. An inch and a half in diameter.

Hab. Found in all parts of the world. It is especially abundant in the neighbourhood of gardens.

H. POMATIA. *Linnæus*. Pl. V, fig. 17.

Shell globose, solid, a tawny colour, with rufous bands, coarsely wrinkled; aperture roundish lunate.

This shell which is generally known by the appellation of "the edible snail," is found in the south of England, and is by some considered a dainty dish. It is principally used as a substitute for animal food during lent. The Romans were particularly fond of them, and probably introduced them into this island from the neighbouring continent, they had their *cochlearia* (snailleries), where they were regularly fattened with new wine boiled down with meal, and probably grew to a much larger size than those found now within our limits, which live on a much scantier and plainer fare. The diameter of a full grown specimen rarely exceeds two inches.

Hab. The southern and midland counties of England, upon cretaceous soils, principally in moss.

H. ARBUSTORUM. *Linnæus.* Pl. VI, fig. 5.

Shell nearly globular, spire more or less elevated; a brown colour beautifully marbled, marked with a single band; outer lip white and reflected.

This is one of the most elegant of our Helices. In shape it approaches *nemoralis,* but is considerably higher and blunter in the spire, with a much smaller mouth in comparison to its size, the lip being also more reflected, and generally extremely white and clear, forms a beautiful contrast with the darker colour of the shell. The inimitable variety of stripes and spots which is seen on its surface will readily distinguish it from the rest. The shell also is thicker than most species. The variation in size, shape, and colour, is very considerable, it is most commonly of a dark chocolate brown mingled with lighter shades, but in the dales of Westmorland they are found of a light yellowish colour, still the distinctive nature of the markings and the peculiar contour of the shell is the same. We have found several specimens with elongated spires, which we considered as monstrosities. About three quarters of an inch in diameter.

Hab. Generally distributed, throughout moist woods and river sides, in most parts of the British Isles.

H. CANTIANA. *Montagu.* Pl. VI, fig. 9.

Shell slightly depressed, subglobose, rufous below and near the mouth; lip not so perceptible as in most of the species of this genus; umbilicus not large.

Helix Carthusiana, *Drap., &c.*

This shell is pretty generally distributed over the country, being found most abundant perhaps in Kent and Sussex, frequently on the sand hills near the sea shores, seeming to prefer the stunted grass and herbage of such places, to the rank luxuriant vegetation of woods and hedge-rows. It may readily be distinguished from its congeners by its greater transparency, and delicate roseate hue. The one most nearly resembling it is *Carthusiana*, which is much smaller; but need never be mistaken for the young of *Cantiana*, since in the latter case, the mouth would not be fully formed until it arrived at its perfect development. About three quarters of an inch in length.

Hab. The recorded localities are "districts around London, and the south of the Thames." They are also found locally abundant in the south of Yorkshire, near Pontefract, near Thirsk, &c., and on the banks of the Tees.

H. CARTHUSIANA. *Muller.* Pl. VI, fig. 12.

Shell depressed, mouth marginated, with a white band; whitish horn colour; umbilicus small.

Helix Carthusianella, *Drap.*, *&c.*

It is very local, being found only on the chalky downs in the south of England, where it sometimes congregates in great numbers, but seldom spreads over a large area. In shape and appearance it most nearly resembles *Cantiana*, but is not half the size, flatter in spire, and of a more delicately pellucid, pinkish white. Diameter about three eighths of an inch.

Hab. Chalky downs in the extreme east of Kent and Surrey.

H. NEMORALIS. *Linnæus.* Pl. VI, fig. 3.

Shell somewhat globose and depressed; variously coloured, often banded; lip reflected, dark brown or black.

This is one of the most variable in colour of land shells, it being difficult to say what is the most prevailing hue. It is very abundant, and may be readily distinguished from the succeeding species by the colour of the lip being a dark brown approaching to black, while *hortensis* is white.

Hab. Found abundantly in all parts of the British Isles; hedge-rows are their favourite resort.

H. HORTENSIS. *Lister.* Pl. VI, fig. 6.

Somewhat globular, thin and smooth; generally of a light yellow colour, with or without bands; lip white.

This shell, unlike *nemoralis*, is very local. It also differs from it in being smaller, not quite so convex, thinner, of a lighter polish, and having the outer lip white, which is a never-failing characteristic. Shell about three quarters of an inch in diameter.

Hab. Woods, hedges, and shady places. We have never met with them except in limestone or sandy districts.

H. HYBRIDA. *Leach*. Pl. VI, fig. 4.

Globular, smooth, glossy, thin; of a purplish brown colour; lip a subdued flesh colour.

This distinct species must have been confounded by several naturalists with some of the many varieties of *nemoralis*. It is invariably of a brownish pink colour, not banded, and has a fleshy pink mouth. Some conchologists suppose it to be a hybrid between *nemoralis* and *hortensis*, hence its name; but there does not seem much ground for such a supposition.

Hab. Under hedge-rows, probably only in limestone districts. Locally abundant. Hackfall woods near Ripon; Hutton Rudby, Cleveland, &c.

H. PISANA. *Muller*. Pl. VI, fig. 8.

Shell white, with numerous interrupted brown bands, both longitudinal and transverse, wrinkled; mouth not large, usually pink edged.

This shell varies much in colour; the bands are sometimes suffused almost over the whole surface, at other times so indistinct as not to be easily detected. It is generally half-an-inch or more in diameter, but varies according to the situation in which it is found.

Hab. Locally very abundant, but is confined to the south-west of England and the south of Ireland; inhabiting dry, sandy plains, near the sea. Tenby, and St. Ives, in Cornwall, are recorded localities.

H. VIRGATA. *Da Costa*. Pl. VI, fig. 10.

Shell white, with one or more brown bands, more or less perceptible; mouth red.

Helix variabilis, *Lam*., *&c*.

If an illustration of the gregarious habits of some of the mollusks is wanted, we could hardly furnish a better example than *H. virgata;* they always live in colonies, and are frequently so numerous, as almost to cover the ground with a mass of animal life. There are many species that have the same congregating habits. It is a variable shell both in size and appearance. Those that most nearly resemble it are *pisana* and *ericetorum;* the former however is larger, generally about twice the size, and may be known by its roseate mouth, and the beautiful checquered stripes that surround it; while the latter has a much flatter spire, and the aperture smaller and more circular. This species seldom attains to half-an-inch in diameter. The spire consists of five whorls, round the base of which the brown band generally winds. The lip is not reflected nor much thicker than the rest of the shell.

Hab. Extremely abundant in chalk and limestone districts, and in sandy places near the sea coast.

H. CAPERATA. *Montagu.* Pl. VI, fig. 15.

Shell a brownish colour, striated; outer whorls rather angular; mouth small and white.

Helix striata, *Drap.*

The name of this shell would seem to premise something beautiful, and we are not disappointed when we find it, but are delighted with its simple elegance of form, and chasteness of colour. There is no other shell that can be confounded with it. The whorls form a regular curve, and do not come to an apex, as most of the other *Helices.* It varies but little in shape, though considerably in colour; the prevailing hue is white, with brown concentrated markings. About three-eighths of an inch in diameter.

Animal a dingy white colour.

Hab. Similar situations to *H. virgata,* may often be met with in large numbers on the sand hills near the sea. Locally abundant.

H. ERICETORUM. *Muller.* Pl. VI, fig. 18.

Shell discoid; white or light brown colour, generally banded; mouth round and small; outer lip acute.

Helix Itala, *Linn.*

This shell may be classed with the former three, in conjunction with which it is frequently found, as having very much the same habits, and living in the same localities. It is generally about three-fourths of an inch in diameter, but varies in size, the average diameter being little more than half an inch. The umbilicus is large and deep. It may be distinguished from *virgata*, in being much more depressed, having the umbilicus much larger and deeper, distinctly exhibiting the second and third whorls, and the outer volution and mouth smaller and more cylindrical; it is also destitute of the rufous colouring within the lip of the shell.

Hab. Limestone districts and sands near the sea. Generally distributed.

H. OBVOLUTA. *Muller*. Pl. VI, fig. 21.

Shell orbicular, a light amber brown colour; spire rather concave; umbilicus spread, deep; lip reflected and white.

This shell does not resemble any of our other British species in appearance, and it is questionable whether it is really indigenous. The aperture is trigonal or foot shaped, with a reflected white lip. It differs from *lapicida*, which is perhaps its nearest ally, in being smaller, of a different colour, having the whorls more clearly defined and concave, and being neither keeled nor much rounded at the circumference. The peculiar shape of the mouth will readily distinguish it from any of the other *Helices*. Diameter nearly half an inch. Animal a dusky colour, head and tentacles black.

Hab. The only recorded localities in which this rare shell has been found, are among moss at the roots of trees in Ditcham Wood, near Brenton, Hants, and along the chalk escarpment of the South Downs.

H. LAPICIDA. *Linnæus*. Pl. VI, fig. 16.

Shell orbicular, depressed; grey or pale rufous, with darker radiations; sharply carinated at the circumference.

The peculiar traits in this shell are, the depressed, and when taken together, regularly curved whorls, the outer one of which is very sharply carinated at the circumference, the purplish rufous colour, and its unpolished surface. Animal a dusky green colour, with two dark streaks running down the back.

Hab. A widely-distributed species, though of necessity local owing to its habits. This is a shell not only peculiar to limestone districts, but to the rocks themselves, in the fissures of which it secretes itself during the drought of summer, and it is only after a period of settled wet weather that it can be found abundantly, even in localities where it is known to be numerous. We can well remember, when taking an excursion in Wensleydale, being very much disappointed at not finding them on the limestone rocks, with the exception of one or two specimens, though we knew they abounded there, a number having been sent us from the same locality, together with the information that they actually swarmed upon the rocks and walls during the wet weather. It has been found on limestone rocks, in Wensleydale, the south of Durham, the south of Yorkshire, and on chalky rocks in the south-east of England.

H. RUFESCENS. *Pennant.* Pl. VI, fig. 19.

Shell depressed, reddish horn colour, concentrically striated, slightly carinated and white at the circumference; umbilicus large.

This shell is generally diffused over England, prefering a chalky soil, where they grow to great perfection. Those found in the north of England are more globular and smaller, seldom being half an inch in diameter, while the typical form, sometimes measures nearly three quarters of an inch. Though the shell varies in colour, it cannot well be confounded with any other species.

Hab. Found in almost every district. Its favourite place of resort, where there are no calcareous rocks, is at the foot of a wall, where they no doubt derive some of their necessary support. More common in the south than the north of England.

H. HISPIDA. *Linnæus.* Pl. VI, fig. 7.

Convex, reddish or brownish horn colour; umbilicus moderately large.

With the exception of some of the *Pisidia*, this is by far the most difficult species to say what are its true limits. Under the name are now included the three distinct species of Gray, *hispida, concinna,* and *depilata.* There is such a difference in the appearance and thickness of the shell that it is very difficult to reconcile them as being the same species. The real *hispida* may be readily distinguished by being thin, and having the periotraca hairy. It most nearly resembles *sericea,* but is of a darker colour and rather more depressed; the animals also are quite distinct.

var. DEPILATA. Shell particularly hard, rather smaller, of a horn colour, more depressed, peristome thickened and of a whitish colour.

It seems to prefer a sandy situation, and is sometimes very abundant on the hillocks near the sea coast.

var. CONCINNA. Shell more nearly approaching *hispida*, and found in similar situations, it differs from it however in having a thicker shell, larger umbilicus, generally more depressed, and is destitute of hairs.

Hab. Woods, either under stones, or climbing up plants and grasses. Common almost everywhere.

H. REVELATA. *Ferussac.* Pl. VI, fig. 22.

Shell globular, thin, diaphanous, shining, pale green colour, downy; umbilicus small.

This shell is by no means common, having been found in a comparatively few places. It is not quite so large as *sericea,* which it most nearly resembles in its general contour, though it may always be distinguished by its peculiar green colour. About a quarter of an inch in diameter.

Hab. The recorded localities are near Doyle's Monument in Guernsey, Torquay, Plymouth, and other places in Devon and Cornwall.

H. SERICEA. *Draparnaud.* Pl. VI, fig. 11.

Somewhat globular, transparent, yellowish horn or white colour, closely downy; six volutions; umbilicus small.

Helix granulata, *Gray, Brown.*

This beautiful little shell may be readily distinguished from *hispida,* which it most nearly resembles, in being a lighter colour, having the hairs finer and more closely set, and the spire not nearly so much depressed. The animal is greyish about the head and tentacles, the mantle marbled with black. This species includes *sericea* and *granulata* of Gray, which appear to be but variations of the same shell, probably arising from some natural or local circumstances. Diameter the third of an inch.

Hab. Found in similar situations to *hispida*; delighting in luxuriant vegetation in damp woods, &c. The species is widely distributed but local, we have met with it abundantly in woods near Middleton-one-row, Durham, and in Bilsdale, Cleveland. It is recorded as being frequent in the south and west of England.

H. LAMELLATA. *Jeffreys.* Pl. VI, fig. 13.

Shell small, trochiform, with close set longitudinal lamellæ; mouth lunate; umbilicus deep.

The similarity between this species and *fulva,* is greater than between it and *aculeata,* though perhaps more properly speaking it holds an intermediate place between the two; the whorls are not so close as those of *fulva,* and it is not so conical, being much blunter in the spire; moreover it is covered with longitudinal ridges, and has a round instead of a flat bottom. About the tenth of an inch in diameter.

Hab. This shell is far from common, having only been found in few localities; it prefers a damp situation amongst decaying vegetable matter. It is confined to the north of England, but generally distributed over Ireland. We have found it in Airy Holme Wood, Cleveland, and other places.

H. aculeata. *Muller*. Pl. VI, fig. 17.

Shell minute, rather trochiform; four volutions, with spines around the upper part of the middle of them.

This is much more common than the preceding, and is found in somewhat similar localities, though it also frequents drier situations. The beautiful rows of spines with which this is fringed, are a peculiar and unique feature, being dispersed in regular rows, and are very large in comparison with the shell. The aperture is nearly round. About the tenth of an inch in diameter. Animal a peculiar grey colour.

Hab. Woods, among leaves and under stones. A bunch of moss from a hedge bank will sometimes yield a number of specimens. It is widely distributed, but scarce in some localities.

H. fulva. *Muller*. Pl. VI, fig. 14.

Shell small, trochiform, smooth and glossy; dark horn colour.

This shell and the two preceding have many characteristics in common, being all of them more or less of a trochoid conical form, with but small apertures. *H. fulva* differs from *aculeata* and *lamellata* in having no spines; being perfectly smooth and shining. The whorls are so close and intimately connected as to give the appearance of a perfect cone with a flat base. It is somewhat larger than the former two, being about the sixth of an inch in diameter. Animal grey with long tentacles.

Hab. It is found in damp places upon stones at the roots of grass and amongst dead and decaying vegetable matter. Widely diffused.

H. fusca. *Montagu*. Pl. VI, fig. 24.

Shell subglobose, transparent, horn colour, wrinkled, very thin; umbilicus narrow.

There is no other species with which this can be confounded, *H. revelata* approaches nearest in form, but is much smaller and of a decidedly green colour, whereas *fusca* is of a delicate straw yellow, exceedingly thin, and moderately transparent. About three-eighths of an inch in diameter. Animal of a yellowish colour, with dusky tentacles, the anterior ones being rather long.

Hab. It is one that loves a luxuriant vegetation, in damp shady woods, where the undergrowth of ferns, nettles, and plants, flourish in unrestrained profusion. It is consequently local, there being few recorded localities, and these chiefly in the north. We have met with it abundantly in Airy Holme Wood,* near Great Ayton, and also in woods near Doncaster, &c. It is peculiar to Britain.

H. PULCHELLA. *Muller.* Pl. VI, fig. 20.

Shell minute, opaque white, depressed; mouth nearly circular, with the lip much reflected.

This little shell well deserves the name of "fair," for though so small it is indeed a lovely gem, of a delicate pellucid white colour; its shape reminding us of the *Carocollæ,* which are found in warmer climates. The large reflected outer lip is very peculiar and gives it an elegant though unsymmetrical appearance, difficult to describe. The umbilicus is large, exposing the upper volutions. Animal white, upper tentacles long and cylindrical.

var. COSTATA, which is grooved longitudinally, is by many marked as a distinct species, but its characteristics do not warrant any such separation.

Hab. It is by no means abundant, but is pretty generally scattered over the country. Its most favourite resorts are rocks and stones, just beneath the surface of the ground, where the roots of grass come in contact with them. The variety is not so common as the normal form, it is recorded as being most abundant at Minching Hampton, near Exeter, on dry walls amongst *Sedum acre.*

H. ROTUNDATA. *Muller.* Pl. VI, fig. 23.

Shell depressed, deeply marked with striæ, rufous, spotted with chocolate; umbilicus very large.

* For an account of the Land Shells found in this wood, see "The Naturalist" for 1854.

Helix radiata, *Da Costa, &c.* Zonites rotundatus, *Gray, &c.*

This common but pretty little shell, is found in almost every locality, and cannot well be mistaken for any other. Its most peculiar characteristic are the radiated striæ, which are very conspicuous. It is abundant in almost every locality, being found in conjunction with *Zonites* and *Zua lubrica*. By some conchologists, this and the following have been classed with the genus *Zonites*, but have more relations in common with the *Helices*. Though the shells of *H. rotundata* are pretty much of one shape and colour, they admit of one or two distinct varieties, which are not so common as the normal species.

var. Turtoni, has the spire quite flattened.

Hab. At the roots of grass, or under stones, in woods, fields or lanes. Abundant all over the British Isles. A pellucid variety, *translucens,* is recorded as having been found at Kenilworth Castle, and other places; it is by no means common.

H. umbilicata. *Montagu.* Pl. VI, fig. 25.

Shell small, wrinkled, opaque, not smooth; aperture circular; outer lip acute; umbilicus very large.

Zonites umbilicatus, *Gray.*

This shell resembles the former in many points, but is much smaller, has a more elongated spire, is not so common, and is found in dry situations. It delights in exposed places, such as the tops of houses or walls. The spire varies, being more elevated in some than others. They show a preference, but are not peculiar to calcareous soils. The colour of the shell is very similar to darker specimens of *rotundata,* as are also the wrinkles or striæ on its surface. Diameter about the tenth of an inch. Animal dark grey, and polished.

Hab. Dry soils, on walls or buildings, in exposed situations. Generally diffused over the British Isles, and very abundant in some places.

H. PYGMÆA. *Draparnaud.* Pl. VI, fig. 34.

Shell minute, rather convex, of a pale brown colour; umbilicus large.

Zonites pygmæus, *Gray*.

This shell differs from the former in being smaller, having the spire much more depressed, being more transparent, and of a pale colour. It is like the former marked with regular longitudinal striæ. Whorls three and a half to four, which are deeply defined. Diameter less than one line.

Hab. There is every reason to believe this delicate little shell is generally diffused over the British Isles; but on account of its being so very minute, and of a colour generally resembling the soil it inhabits, it probably has been overlooked in many districts. Unlike the former species, it delights in damp situations, amongst dried leaves and decayed vegetable matter. Often found at the roots of grass in a moderately damp field.

We reject *H. limbata* as spurious, on the authority of Professor Forbes and S. Hanley. It is a continental species. The few specimens which have been found, were probably introduced with foreign plants.

BULIMUS. *Scopoli.*

Shell—*Spiral, oblong, unpolished, aperture oval, devoid of teeth; columella entire.*

Animal—*Similar to that of Helix.*

B. ACUTUS. *Muller.* Pl. VII, fig. 1.

Turreted, conical, white or clear brown, generally banded; peristome thin, scarcely reflected.

This beautiful turreted little snail is gregarious in its habits, and locally distributed, being partially if not exclusively confined to calcareous soils. It varies much in colour, being sometimes nearly white and sometimes a light brown, in both cases with the bands more or less perceptible. It is very similar to *virgata* in its habits. Indeed the distinction between the *Bulimi* and *Helices* is nothing more than a little difference in the conformation of the shell. Length usually about half an inch. Animal yellowish, with four tentacles, upper one long.

Hab. Extremely abundant in the west and south of England, on chalk or sandy maratime pastures. It is also recorded as having been found on the Isle of Man, in the west of Scotland and Hebrides, and many parts of Ireland.

B. Lackhamensis. *Montagu.* Pl. VII, fig. 2.

Shell oblong, chocolate brown colour; mouth sub-oval.

Bulimus montanus, *Brown, &c.*

This fine *Bulimus,* which is found only in the south of England, is probably, like the former species, confined to the chalk and limestone formations. It is one of our rarest land shells, having been found in comparatively few localities. The equal coating of chocolate brown colour, together with its size, about five-eighths of an inch in length, and spiral appearance, readily distinguish it. The animal resembles that of *obscurus.*

Hab. Wooded districts in the south of England, on the lime and chalk formation, frequently on the stems of trees, beech trees in particular, or under decayed leaves at their roots. Essex, Kent, Wiltshire, Somersetshire, and many localities near Cheltenham, are recorded.

B. obscurus. *Muller.* Pl. VII, fig. 3.

Shell similarly shaped to the last, but smaller; brownish horn colour; peristome white, reflected.

Helix obscura, *Gmel., &c.*

This shell closely resembles the preceding species, but is smaller, being little more than three lines and a half long; the volutions are somewhat more rounded, the mouth shorter, and peristome white. The colour is much lighter and devoid of the dark brown or chocolate hue. The greatest peculiarity about this shell is that it envelopes itself with a coating of mud, seemingly for the purpose of escaping detection; hence its name "obscurus," When it is found on the trunks of trees, the colour of its coat generally partakes of that of the part it is on. The animal is very similar to the preceding.

Hab. Hedges, amongst dead leaves, under stones, &c.; and in woods, frequently on the stems of trees. It is widely diffused, being found more or less abundantly in all parts of the British Isles.

The spurious species *B. Goodalli*, *B. decollatus*, and *B. clavulus*, have been introduced by some naturalists into the British Fauna, from living specimens having been found in pine-beds, warmed by artificial heat, at Bristol, Exeter, and other places.

PUPA. *Lamark.*

Shell—*Spiral, more or less cylindrical, abruptly obtuse; whorls numerous and close; mouth mostly toothed within, peristome reflected.*

Animal—*Short, four tentacles, the upper ones developed, the lower ones short, sometimes hardly discernible.*

P. UMBILICATA. *Draparnaud.* Pl. VII, fig. 4.

Cylindrical, brownish; mouth lunate, provided with one tooth; peristome much reflected.

This is the commonest, though by no means the least attractive of the *Pupæ;* its little ivory white lip forming a beautiful contrast with the body of the shell, which is of a dark chocolate colour, and polished. It approaches nearest in form to *muscorum*, being about the same size, and having a single tooth on the pillar; but differs in having the whorls more loosely set, and more inclined to the axis. The peristome too, is not only thickened but reflected; whilst the lip of *muscorum*, although thickened is not reflected. It is also a brighter colour, and somewhat pellucid. The animal is of a lead colour above, and white beneath; the upper tentacles long, lower ones short but distinct.

Hab. This shell is very plentiful; inhabiting chiefly woods and hedge-rows, among the roots of grass or dead leaves. Another favourite habitat are the fissures found in the bark of such trees as the oak, where it may be sometimes found in considerable numbers, clustered together; the moss and lichen which cover them may also often be searched with success. It is a widely distributed species, and found in all parts of the British Isles.

P. MUSCORUM. *Linnæus.* Pl. VII, fig. 5.

Shell, cylindrical, yellowish brown or chestnut colour; outer lip not reflected, but margined by a strong external rib.

Pupa marginata, *Drap.*, *&c.*

There is very little difference between this and the former species, as noticed above; the chief point of distinction is in the outer lip, which is here curiously marginated by a strong rounded callus or rib. The spine consists of six or seven volutions; the basal one is not so much extended as in *umbilicata.* The shell is moderately strong, not diaphanous or shining, of a yellow or brown colour, and slightly striated. Animal greyish black, white underneath, lower tentacles very short.

Hab. It is often found in similar localities to the last, but may be also found in dryer situations, on sands near the sea, or calcareous soils. It is widely distributed.

P. ANGLICA. *Ferussac.* Pl. VII, fig. 6.

Shell dextral, shining dark brown approaching to black; peristome flatly reflected; mouth with fine teeth.

This beautiful little shell is somewhat smaller than the preceding, and may be readily distinguished from them by having its mouth thickly set with five little threatening teeth. Its colour also is much darker, being almost black. The aperture is something of the shape of the lobe of the human ear. Animal dark lead colour above, white beneath.

Hab. It is quite a local shell, and may almost be *considered rare,* having only been found in a few places in the north of England and part of Ireland. Scarbro', near Newcastle, Airy Holme Wood in Cleveland, and Hackfall Woods near Ripon, are some of the recorded localities. It seems to delight in deep, shady, somewhat boggy and peaty woods, living amongst the rankly growing weeds, which flourish upon soil formed from decomposed vegetable matter.

P. SECALE. *Draparnaud.* Pl. VII, fig. 7.

Shell rather cylindrical, dextral, brown; aperture with seven or eight teeth; peristome acute.

Pupa juniperi, *Gray, &c.*

This largest of the *Pupa* genus is found almost exclusively in the south of England, and is readily distinguished both from its size and the number of laminar teeth within the aperture. Of a dull brown or pale chocolate brown colour. Whorls from seven to nine in number. It generally measures about a quarter of an inch in length. Animal blackish brown above, pale beneath.

Hab. Limestone localities in the south of England. Headington Quarry near Oxford, and limestone in the neighbourhood of Kendal. Roots of trees and under stones, &c.

P. EDENTULA. *Draparnaud.* Pl. VII, fig. 8.

Minute, dextral; mouth toothless; peristome simple, not reflected.

Vertigo edentula, *Gray, &c.*

This *Pupa* may be readily distinguished from the other by the number of volutions, which in full grown specimens are six or seven in number, and its cylindrical shape, in which characteristic it closely resembles *minutissima*, from which it may be distinguished by its greater size. The lip has no external rib or callus, nor is it at all reflected. The shell is transparent, of a light horn colour, very thin and somewhat polished. Length rather more than the tenth of an inch, and height about one third the length. The animal is grey above but lighter beneath.

Hab. Damp places at the roots of grass, under stones, &c. It is widely diffused, but rather local. This, together with the remaining members of the *Pupa* genus, may have been overlooked on account of their being so minute, and their colour so often resembling that of the soil, leaves, &c., on which they may be found. Plentiful in many parts of Yorkshire and Durham.

P. MINUTISSIMA. *Hartmann.* Pl. VII, fig. 9.

Shell minute, cylindrical, dextral, a pale brown colour, wrinkled; mouth edentulous; lips scarcely reflected.

Pupa muscorum, *Drap.* Vertigo cylindrica, *Gray.*

With the exception of *Venetzii*, this is the rarest of our British Pupæ. It may easily be distinguished by its minute size, not measuring more than one line in length, by two-fifths of a line in breadth, and cylindrical shape. Whorls five or five and a half, much rounded; suture abrupt. The animal is dark, streaked with black and shining.

Hab. There is every reason to believe this somewhat rare *Pupa* is generally diffused through the British Isles. It seems partial to calcareous rocks, and the debris at their base may often be searched with success. The reported localities are Balmenna, Fifeshire, Durdham Downs near Bristol, and Salisbury Crags, Edinburgh. We have also found it pretty abundantly in conjunction with *pusilla, edentula, substriata, pygmæa,* and many commoner shells, upon the top of the magnesian limestone crags, Went Vale near Ackworth.

P. PYGMÆA. *Druparnaud.* Pl. VII, fig. 10.

Shell minute, dextral, ovate; whorls four to five; mouth with four or five teeth; peristome marginated externally.

Vertigo pygmæa, *Gray, &c.*

In shape and external characteristics, this little shell somewhat resembles *substriata*, but the latter is more conical, and has six teeth; it is also rather less. The peristome of *pygmæa* is slightly thickened and reflexed. Animal dark grey, upper tentacles small, lower ones almost obsolete.

var. ALPESTRIS, *Forbes and Hanley*, has only four teeth, it may also be distinguished by its lighter colouring, and more cylindrical shape.

Hab. Widely distributed, and in some places abundant; under stones, decayed leaves, &c. The variety has, as yet, been found only in the northern counties.

P. SUBSTRIATA, *Jeffreys*. Pl. VII, fig. 11.

Shell minute, dextral, striated; mouth with six teeth (only four easily perceptible); yellow horn colour.

Vertigo substriata, *Gray*. Turbo sexdentatus, *Mont*.

This minute shell is more conical than the preceding, and longitudinally striated. The volutions, four or five in number, are well rounded and rather high. It may be distinguished by being the smallest of the tribe, and having the two parietal teeth very perceptible. Animal blackish grey.

Hab. Like most of the other shells of this genus, particularly the *Vertigo* section of them, it seems to be widely distributed, but often overlooked on account of its diminutive size, &c. Among wet moss or grass, in marshy places. The principal localities in which it has been found are in the north of England, but Norfolk and Devonshire are also recorded districts. We have observed it among peaty soil, on magnesian limestone rocks in the south of Yorkshire.

P. ANTIVERTIGO. *Draparnaud*. Pl. VII, fig. 12.

Shell dextral, minute, shining brown, with five volutions; mouth trigonally lunate, with from seven to nine teeth.

Vertigo palustris, *Gray*.

This beautiful little *Pupa* is easily distinguished from the rest; firstly by its shining dark chocolate colour, with the extreme margin of the aperture whitish; secondly by its teeth, three of which are very prominent and easily perceived, they are of unequal size;

and thirdly by the peculiar localities which it frequents. The whorls are five in number, quickly enlarging, which gives it an oval, or irregular spindle shape. Animal dark, shining; upper tentacles thick and short, lower ones almost imperceptible, mere dots.

Hab. Marshes and other wet places; the muddy sides of slow streams, canals, &c. It is widely distributed, rather local, but sometimes plentiful. It has been found near Swansea, Bath, Bristol, Cheltenham, &c.; also near Oxford and many places in the south of England.

P. PUSILLA. *Muller.* Pl. VII, fig. 13.

Shell cylindrical, minute; mouth sinistral, with six to eight teeth; peristome thin.

Vertigo pusilla, *Gray.*

By being sinistral this shell is at once distinguished from the remainder of the genus, except *Venetzii*, from which it may be distinguished by being much larger, and having the aperture larger, and of a semi-oval shape. *Pusilla* is transparent, glossy, and of a pale chestnut colour. The mouth is armed with six or seven teeth, and one is sometimes appended to the pillar lip. Animal dark grey, pale underneath.

Hab. Among damp moss, under stones, &c. It is widely diffused, and in some places pretty abundant. Walls at Woodeaton, near Oxford, and many other districts in the southern and eastern counties; Went Vale, near Ackworth, and other localities in Durham, Northumberland, and Westmoreland. Rare in Ireland.

P. VENETZII. *Charpentier.* Pl. VII, fig. 14.

Shell very minute, sinistral, pale amber colour, teeth four or five.

Vertigo angustior, *Gray.* Turbo vertigo, *Mont.*

This rare shell has only been discovered in a few localities, in the British Isles. It is very minute, thin, and not shining. Its little, short, thick-set whorls, which are abruptly terminated at the apex and contracted at the base, give it a peculiar barrel-like appearance. The mouth is very small and of a curious subtriangular shape. We have not seen a living specimen of this shell, nor any description of the animal.

Hab. The recorded localities are the rejectment of a small stream at Merino, near Swansea, Cork, and Miltown Malbay in Clare. We have also found it amongst the rejectment of a small stream running into the Tees, near Norton.

BALEA. *Prideux.*

Shell—*Sinistral, regular, elongated, tapering, oval; spire resembling Clausilia, but has no clausium; a single tooth on the pillar.*

Animal—*Resembling Bulimus.*

B. FRAGILIS. *Draparnaud.* Pl. VII, fig. 15.

Turbo perversus, *Linn.* Pupa fragilis, *Drap.* Clausilia fragilis, *Jeff.* Balea perversa, *Gray.*

This genus is intermediate between *Pupa* and *Clausilia;* from the former it differs in the unequal margin of the mouth, and from the latter in having no clausium, and the last whorl larger than the others. From *Bulimus* it differs in having the aperture sinistral. It is semi-transparent, and of a yellow olivaceous colour. Whorls six or seven, slanting regularly to the apex, which is rather acute. This shell closely resembles the young of *Clausilia nigricans,* but may be distinguished from it by having the last whorl convex, not flattened or keeled. Aperture pyriform. About the third of an inch in length. Animal dark grey, rather mottled.

Hab. Found in all parts of the British Isles; on the trunks of trees, sometimes under moss, lichens, &c., which are attached to walls. It is probably one of the many shells which prefer limestone districts.

CLAUSILIA. *Draparnaud.*

Shell—*Spiral, produced, the last volution less turned than the one before it, sinistral; aperture pyriform, toothed; throat closed by an internal testaceous plate or clausium.*

Animal—*Short; upper tentacles stout, lower ones very small.*

The great peculiarity in these shells is the clausium, which is thus described by Gray. "It consists of a spirally-twisted thin shelly plate, inclosed in the last whorl of the shell. When the animal is retracted within its shell, this shelly plate nearly covers the aperture at a little distance within the mouth, and coming in contact with a transverse plait on the outer lip, leaves only a small canal formed between the outer plait and the posterior angle of the mouth, and sometimes an elongated longitudinal plait on the inner lip. When the animal wishes to protrude itself, it pushes the plate on one side into a grove situated between the inner plait and the columella, where it is detained by the pressure of the body of the animal, leaving the aperture free; and when the animal withdraws itself, the plate springs forward by the elasticity of the pedicle and closes the aperture."

C. LAMINATA. *Montagu.* Pl. VI, fig. 27.

Shell large, nearly smooth, glossy, and semi-transparent.

Clausilia bidens, *Gray, &c.*

This large *Clausilia* sometimes measures three quarters of an inch in length. The shell is generally of a brownish colour and smooth, except at the base of the last whorl, which is slightly striated. Transparent greenish white specimens are sometimes, though rarely, to be met with. Whorls ten, slightly convex; the suture is distinct but not deep. The peristome thick and whitish, not reflexed, of a pyriform shape; the upper plate is small and straight, the under one, which is in the middle of the pillar lip, curved. The animal brownish, the upper tentacles clavate.

Hab. This shell is more common in the south than

in the north of England. It shows a great partiality to beech woods, living among the decayed leaves of that tree, and may sometimes be found on the trunk of the tree itself.

C. BIPLICATA. *Montagu.* Pl. VI, fig. 28.

Shell ventricose, dark greyish brown, with regular longitudinal striæ; aperture with two plates.

Clausilia ventricosa, *Jeff.*, *&c.*

The regular raised striæ at once distinguishes this shell from the former, which it most nearly resembles in other particulars. The spire consists of from ten to twelve depressed, convex, but well-defined volutions; aperture sub-pyriform, with two plates, and sometimes one or two additional denticles. It is about two thirds or three quarters of an inch in length.

Hab. This beautiful *Clausilia* is confined to the south of England, inhabiting woods and hedges near London; it has also been found at Bristol. It is probably confined to the chalk districts. By no means common.

C. PLICATULA. *Draparnaud.* Pl. VI, fig. 29.

Shell ventricose, thin, opaque; with regular longitudinal raised striæ; aperture containing four or five plates.

Clausilia Rolphii, *Gray.*

This rare *Clausilia* may be distinguished from *biplicata* by its reddish chocolate brown colour, and by the plates within the aperture. The costella striæ are fine and only slightly raised. Whorls ten to twelve, moderately well defined, but not particularly convex. From three-fifths to three quarters of an inch in length. Animal dark grey, upper tentacles thick and clavate.

Hab. First discovered by Rolph, in Charlton Wood, Kent. It has since been found in other localities in Kent; also near Hastings, in Hampshire, Dovedale, in the Marsh, Gloucestershire, and Birdlip to Cooper's Hill, near Cheltenham. It prefers damp situations at the root of *Mercurialis perennis, saxifraga oppositifolia* and other plants, on a chalky soil.

C. NIGRICANS. *Maton and Rackett.* Pl. VI, fig. 30.

Shell slender, opaque, dark brown; five more or less raised, somewhat granular, striæ; mouth with three plates, margin white.

Clausilia rugosa, *Brown.*

This is by far the commonest of our British Clausilia, being abundant almost everywhere. It may readily be distinguished from the others by being so much less, seldom attaining half-an-inch in length. It is nearly opaque with a dark brown lustre, often marked with whitish streaks. The spire is composed of from seven to eleven moderately convex volutions. Aperture small and pyriform.

var. DUBIA, (Plate VI, fig. 31,) is somewhat larger, more ventricose; the striæ broader and more raised.

Hab. Plentiful in almost every locality in the British Isles. It may be found under stones on walls and rocks (particularly limestone), in the earth or even on trees. The variety occurs in the north-east of England. Tanfield, near Ripon, Haughton-le-spring, near Sunderland, &c.; it has been found as far south as Oxford.

ZUA. *Leach.*

Shell—*Spiral, rather cylindrical, blunt, smooth and polished; mouth ovate; peristome toothless, thickened but not reflexed.*

Animal—*Allied to and closely resembling Bulimus.*

Z. LUBRICA. *Muller.* Pl. VI, fig. 32.

Helix lubrica, *Mont.* Bulimus lubricus, *Brown.*

At first sight there is a considerable likeness between this species and *Azeca tridens*, but its lighter colour, slender shape, and more prominent whorls will readily distinguish it; besides the never-failing characteristic, the mouth, which in this shell is almost oval, quite plain, and not furnished with projections as in *A. tridens*. This genus is distinguished from *Bulimus* by its polished periostraca. The shell varies in size and colour, though generally an olivaceous brown; it is highly polished and transparent. Length a quarter of an inch. Animal dark grey above, lighter underneath, upper tentacles nearly black, and clavate.

Hab. It has a very wide distribution, and may be found in almost every situation where vegetation of any kind flourishes. Fields, hedge-rows, woods, and waste places, amongst the roots of grass or moss, stones, or buried an inch or two in the earth. Very abundant.

AZECA. *Leach.*

Shell—*Spiral, subcylindrical, smooth, remarkably shining; aperture pyriform; peristome entire, thick and toothed, not reflexed.*

Animal—*Like that of Zua.*

A. TRIDENS. *Pulteney.* Pl. VI, fig. 33.

Turbo tridens, *Mont.*

Shell ovate, cylindrical, firmer than the preceding, brightly polished and of a reddish brown colour; smooth, with the exception of a few wrinkles near the suture. Whorls seven or eight and much depressed. Mouth small and pyriform, guarded by three prominent teeth, sometimes two additional small ones intervening. It may readily be distinguished from its congeners by its shining barrel-like form, with whorls scarcely projecting at all, and its contracted mouth protected by threatening teeth. Length about a quarter of an inch. Animal dark.

Hab. This pretty little shell is generally distributed over the country, and though by no means uncommon, is much more local than the preceding. Its usual habitat is amongst the damp and luxuriantly growing vegetation of woods. It is one of the mollusks which seem to live in colonies, so that the collector may be pretty certain when he finds one or two specimens, that there are a number not far distant. It has not yet been found in Ireland.

Achatina. *Leach.*

Shell—*Spiral, elongated; mouth ovate or elongated; peristome thin, never reflexed.*

Animal—*Closely resembling that of Bulimus.*

A. acicula. *Muller.* Pl. VII, fig. 16.

Bulimus acicula, *Drap.*, *&c.*

Shell about a quarter of an inch long, tapering, acute at the apex, narrow in proportion to the length. Outer margin of the lip thin, not reflexed, of a uniform white colour, smooth and polished. Pillar smooth, simple, curved and truncated in front. Animal white, upper tentacles cylindrical, not thickened at the extremity, and deprived of eyes. This genus approaches in form and appearance to the *Bulimus*, but may be distinguished from it by the mouth being at least half the length of the entire shell. They are a most interesting genus, many of those found in tropical countries attain to a large size, so that we can have little idea of them from their tiny representative in the British Isles.

Hab. This delicate shell delights in a sandy soil, taking up its quarters among the roots of grass. The downs and hillocks near the coast may be frequently searched with success. After a considerable flood we once found them in great abundance amongst the rejectment of the river Tees, near Middlesbro', whence they had been brought from the banks of the stream higher up. Living specimens are comparatively rare. In many places it must be regarded as subfossil; it appears to have abounded in Britian at the close of the tertiary epoch.

Succinea. *Draparnaud.*

Shell—*Oblong, oval, thin, spire conical, body whorl very large; mouth oblong; peristome thin; pillar smooth.*

Animal—*Large, upper tentacles short and reflexed, lower ones very short.*

S. PUTRIS. *Linnæus.* Pl. VII, fig. 18.

Oblong, reddish amber colour, spire consisting of three whorls, small; aperture oblique.

Helix putris, *Mont.* Succinea amphibia, *Drap.* Succinea gracilis, *Brown, &c.*

Naturalists have found some difficulty in describing and affording limits to the species under this genus, especially in regard to this particular member. It comprises, under the present arrangement, two distinct species of Gray, *S. putris* and *Pfeifferi,* as it is considered that the localities in which they are found, have sufficient influence on their nature to account for the difference between them. The shell of the normal form is large, sometimes attaining three quarters of an inch in length; the colour varies from a rufous amber to a pale yellow. The surface is glossy and more or less wrinkled. Animal grey, spotted; tentacles rugose. On account of the diversities of form, &c., which this shell assumes, is has been split up into many varieties.

var. AMPHIBIA is more compressed, and has the sutures more oblique. The whorls, scarcely three in number, are flattened above and rounded below, the apex being very minute. Fine specimens are about half-an-inch in length.

The other forms are *gracilis,* oval, more or less swollen, of a more pallid and less rufous colour than the preceding. Its whorls typically much rounded; its sutures not peculiarly oblique: and its spire never elongated. *Intermedia* presents the modified peculiarities of the preceding extreme forms; there are three and a half coils, so that the spire is occasionally more elongated in proportion than *gracilis* or *amphibia.*

Hab. Abundant in almost every locality. S. *Putris* inhabiting damp woods and meadows, while *amphibia* prefers a still damper situation, and is never found except on aquatic plants and mud by the sides of slow running streams, ditches, &c., frequently immersed in the water.

S. oblonga. *Draparnaud.* Pl. VII, fig. 19.

Shell ovate; whorls three or four, produced, ventricose; aperture ovate.

This rare British *Succinea,* may be readily distinguished from *putris,* by being much smaller, seldom measuring more than a quarter of an inch in length, having the spire more produced, and the aperture nearly oval, and about equal to the spire in length. Animal blackish grey, with paler thick set tentacles.

Hab. Edge of ditches, &c. It was found near Swansea, but we have been told that it is now extinct in that locality; the only place in which it appears to have been found in England is at "Topsham, Exeter, three or four specimens in salt water marshes." It has been found in several places in Ireland, and near Glasgow, in Scotland. Sometimes found in superficial deposits, half fossilized.

LIMNÆADÆ.

Physa. *Draparnaud.*

Shell—*Thin, spiral, sinistral, polished; mouth oblong.*
Animal—*Tentacles long, with eyes at their bases.*

The British species of this genus have been formerly referred to two genera, *Physa* and *Aplexus.* The animal of the former has a dilated mantle with lobed edges; that of the latter has a simple mantle.

P. fontinalis. *Linnæus.* Pl. VII, fig. 20.

Shell oval, horn coloured; spire very short and obtuse; aperture much dilated.

Bulla fontinalis, *Linn.*, *&c.*

This pretty shell which is commonly called "The Bubble Shell," is common throughout the greater part of the British Isles. It varies much in form, and has been separated into a great many varieties by some naturalists. It may be easily distinguished by its exceedingly small spire, its regular oval form, its thin glossy and almost smooth exterior, together with its yellowish horn colour. It often attains to the third of an inch in length, the breadth being nearly one-fourth. Animal lighter or darker grey, with long slender tentacles of a paler colour.

var. ACUTA is larger and narrower, with a more elongated spire. This variety is by no means common. The variety 2 of Gray has the last whorl rather angular behind, it is smaller than the normal form, and recorded as being found "in very small plashes of water or in water among grass." The difference of situation is probably sufficient to account for the variations.

Hab. Streams, pools, &c., on aquatic plants in all parts of the British Isles.

P. HYPNORUM. *Linnæus.* Pl. VII, fig. 26.

Shell oblong, conical; spire elongated and acute; aperture oval lanceolate.

Bulla hypnorum, *Mont.* Aplexus hypnorum, *Gray.*

This shell is in many respects similar to the preceding, but differs from it in having a more elongated spire, the last volution of which is not so ventricose. The whorls are depressed, glossy, and transparent. Aperture lanceolate ovate. About half-an-inch in length, and one-fifth of an inch in breadth. Animal nearly black, foot long and lanceolate.

Hab. Ditches, ponds, and slow running streams throughout the British Isles, except the extreme north of Scotland. It is as common, though somewhat more local than the preceding.

PLANORBIS. *Muller.*

Shell—*Spiral, discoid, dextral ; aperture lunate, margin entire ; peristome simple, neither thickened nor reflexed.*

Animal—*A broad head with two tentacles, having eyes at their inner bases ; foot small.*

P. CORNEUS. *Linnæus.* Pl. VII, fig. 17.

Shell large, nearly flat above, deeply umbilicate beneath; whorls five, wrinkled, deeply divided, convex above, flattened beneath; aperture semicircular.

Helix cornea, *Mont.*, *&c.*

This largest of our British *Planorbes* cannot possibly be confused with any other on account of its superior size, often measuring one inch in diameter, and one-third of an inch in height. The shell is strong, generally of a rusty brown or olivaceous yellow colour; it is closely and obliquely striate. The animal is nearly black, and when irritated gives out a purple fluid.

Hab. This elegant shell seems to hold a similar position among the *Planorbes*, to that of *H. pomatia* among the *Helices*, both being considerably larger than any other species belonging to the same genus. It is abundant in canals, ponds, slowly-running streams, &c., in all parts of the south of England, with the exception of Cornwall and Devon. It is recorded as having been found as far north as Darlington. It occurs in one or two localities towards the south of Yorkshire and Lancashire. It has been found in Ireland.

P. ALBUS. *Muller.* Pl. VII, fig. 27.

Shell small, white or nearly so; slightly convex on both disks, whorls nearly striated and pilose.

Planorbis hispidus, *Drap.*, *&c.*

This pretty little shell may be instantly detected when quite fresh by its downy appearance, being covered with minute hairs, which fall off with the epidermis. It is the only British fresh-water species that is at all hispid. The shell is thin, not much polished; the upper surface a little sunk in the middle, the lower still more concave; rather angularly rounded at the periphery; about a quarter of inch in diameter. Generally a pale horn colour, but sometimes, particularly old specimens, more or less white. Animal a pale grey, but varies in different localities.

Hab. Stagnant waters upon aquatic plants, *Potamogeton* in particular. It is widely distributed, and may be found more or less sparingly in almost every locality. We have met with them occasionally in several stells, in the neighbourhood of Ayton.

P. GLABER. *Jeffreys.* Pl. VII, fig. 21.

Shell small, whorls equally convex on both sides, round and prominent, the outer one not keeled.

Planorbis lævis, *Gray, &c.*

This little shell somewhat resembles the foregoing, but may be readily distinguished by being smaller, about one-fifth of an inch in diameter, and having the whorls much closer set, and more rounded, especially on the upper disk. It is also destitute of the spiral striæ or hairs.

Hab. Though generally distributed it is somewhat local. It is found in similar habitats to the preceding. It occurs in Cornwall and the south of Wales, Oxfordshire and the adjacent counties, Staffordshire and Somersetshire, North Stainley, near Ripon, and at Ackworth, near Pontefract, in an old depopulated fishpond, on *Potomogeton crispus.* It has also been met with in other places in Yorkshire, Durham, and Northumberland.

P. NAUTILEUS. *Linnæus.* Pl. VII, fig. 23.

Shell minute, with numerous transverse ridges; whorls depressed and keeled; aperture oval.

Planorbis imbricatus, *Mull., &c.*

A beautiful little shell, and may be readily distinguished by the spinous ridges on the outer whorl. From an eighth to a tenth of an inch in diameter. The shell is of an olivaceous horn colour, often covered with a darker epidermis, not polished. Whorls from three to three and a half, which are well defined. Animal pale grey.

Hab. Somewhat local, though generally diffused, and in some places abundant. It prefers stagnant water in ponds, ditches, &c., generally adhering to aquatic plants, often in colonies. Ponds near Ackworth, in profusion, ditches near Middlesbro', &c. It occurs in most parts of Ireland.

P. CARINATUS. *Muller.* Pl. VII, fig. 24.

Shell horn coloured, somewhat transparent and polished, nearly smooth, strongly carinated.

The shell of this species is of an ashy horn colour, often covered with an outer brown epidermis, rather shining and nearly smooth. It is about half-an-inch in diameter with five deeply-divided whorls, which gradually incline to the outer edge, which is more or less keeled. Upper disk rather concave, lower disk flat.

var. DISCIFORMIS, has the lower disk almost convex, and the keel more central.

Hab. Stagnant or slowly-running waters in almost every district, but it is local. More common in the south than the north. Very fine at Norton, near Stockton.

P. MARGINATUS. *Draparnaud.* Pl. VII, fig. 28.

Shell brown colour, slightly concave above, flat beneath, striolate, not polished, carinated.

Helix planorbis, *Linn.*

This species very much resembles the last, but may be distinguished from it by being thicker and having the whorls more rounded, the outer one being more or less carinated near the base, the upper part of which is rounded, not shelving. The mouth is rhombic, but rounded in front. It is covered with an olivaceous black, or ferruginous coating, which is not polished, and distinctly wrinkled. About half-an-inch in diameter.

The shells included under this species vary much both in shape and colour; the keel, which in some specimens is prominent, is scarcely discernible or altogether wanting in others. It has, by some naturalists, been divided into several distinct species.

var. RHOMBEUS, shell higher than usual, with the gyrations rather more compact, more convex above and concave below; keel almost obsolete.

var. DRAPARNALDI, somewhat smaller than the above, and resembles a young *carinatus*.

Hab. This is by far the commonest of the *Planorbes*,

being found abundantly in a number of localities in almost every district, in ponds or ditches of stagnant water, or slowly-running streams and rivers.

P. VORTEX. *Linnæus.* Pl. VII, fig. 30.

Shell depressed, thin, nearly flat above, concave beneath; whorls six or seven, convex above, flat beneath; circumference somewhat carinated.

Helix vortex, *Linn.*

Shell extremely depressed, discoid, about three eighths of an inch in diameter, thin, transparent, and closely wrinkled, of an olivaceous horn colour. The body is broader above than below. Aperture a little angular, broader than long. Volutions slightly concave above, flat underneath, which forms a sharp keel at the base of the periphery. The animal varies in colour, but is generally grey, with darker head. Tentacles long.

Hab. Widely distributed and common in most districts, in ponds, ditches, and canals, preferring those which flow slowly or are quite stagnant.

P. SPIRORBIS. *Linnæus.* Pl. VII, fig. 29.

Shell thin, depressed, concave both above and below; mouth roundish.

Helix spirobis, *Mont., &c.*

Very closely resembling the last species, but may be distinguished by having both disks concave; it is also less, but rather thicker. The body consists of five or six whorls, the outer one of which is not much carinated.

Hab. Very much the same localities and situations as the former; they are very often found in the same pond, though seldom so plentifully.

P. CONTORTUS. *Linnæus.* Pl. VII, fig. 31.

Shell nearly flat above, deeply umbilicate beneath; whorls closely coiled but separated by a deep surture; aperture narrow and crescent-shaped.

Helix contorta, *Linn., &c.*

This pretty little shell cannot possibly be confounded with any of the other species of *Planorbis*. Its whorls are six in number, and extremely narrow, but prominent and well defined. Diameter about one-fifth of an inch, height one tenth. The mouth is peculiarly small and unarmed. Aperture of a narrow crescent shape, only slightly produced on the upper side.

Hab. Widely distributed throughout the British Isles, though absent in some districts. It may generally be found in ponds, ditches, or slow streams.

P. NITIDUS. *Muller.* Pl. VII, fig. 22.

Shell depressed, smooth, polished, transparent, horn coloured, carinated at the periphery, flat above, concave beneath, wrinkled.

Helix fontana, *Light.* Planorbis complanatus, *Drap.*

This shell, which is by no means common, closely resembles the succeeding species, but is more depresed, less polished, pale coloured, and devoid of septa. Whorls more convex and distinct and rather wrinkled; umbilicus much larger. The shell is seldom a quarter of an inch in diameter.

Hab. Though this species is not mentioned in the fauna of several districts, there is reason to believe it is generally distributed through England. We have met with it, but sparingly, in several localities in Yorkshire. in clear stagnant water on acquatic plants.

P. LACUSTRIS. *Lightfoot.* Pl. VII, fig. 25.

Shell highly polished, with internal partitions; whorls flattened; periphery carinated; aperture triangular.

Planorbis nitidus, *Mull.* Sementina lineata, *Flem.*, *Gray.*

This beautiful *Planorbis* is about a quarter of an inch in diameter, and remarkably smooth, shining, and transparent, of an olivaceous brown colour, with white radiations on the outer volution, exhibiting the internal partitions. The upper side is flattened convex, having the middle whorls of the spire thick; the under side flat, with a very small deep umbilicus. Body whorl extremely large filling nearly the whole surface, the circumference of which slopes gradually and rather convexly to an angulated edge, which is below the centre of the shell.

Hab. Somewhat common in the south of England, but becomes more rare towards the north. Its northernmost English locality is near York. It is recorded as occurring in the south of Scotland. Ditches and ponds of stagnant water, containing aquatic plants, are its favourite resorts.

LIMNÆUS. *Draparnaud.*

Shell—*Ovate, dextral, diaphanous; aperture ovate, bounded by an entire margin, without operculum.*

Animal—*With a broad head and compressed tentacles, with eyes at their inner bases; mantle simple.*

L. PEREGER. *Muller.* Pl. VII, fig. 41.

Shell striolate, more or less ventricose; spire short, rather acute; whorls convex.

Helix putris, *Penn.* Limnæus ovatus, *Drap.* Limnæus vulgaris, *Pfeif.*, *&c.*

This commonest of our fluviatile mollusks, is of an infinite variety of forms and shapes; two or three of the principal of which we will endeavour to describe. The shell of the normal form is of a greyish or yellowish colour, thin, not fragile, glossy, concentrically striated; slightly wrinkled longitudinally; spire more or less depressed, consisting of four whorls. Mouth large, oval, oblong, but peaked above; umbilicus small, sometimes nearly obsolete.

var. OVATA. Ventricose, with an acute but exceedingly short spire. Body whorl much expanded, forming a capacious mouth.

var. LINEATA, body large, spire not long, with the apex often corroded; generally of an olivaceous ferruginous colour, the outer whorl lineated.

var. MARGINATA, *Michaud,* has the internal lip of the outer rim thickened.

We have noticed a small variety, *acuta*, with the spire elongated and acute, and the suture more distinct and more oblique; about half an inch in length.

Hab. Common every where, and in all kinds of localities, though it seems to prefer ponds and ditches of stagnant water.

L. AURICULARIUS. *Linnæus.* Pl. VII, fig. 45.

Shell very much inflated, almost as broad as long; spire short and acute; aperture an oblique circular oval, vastly expanded; outer lip patulous.

Helix auricularia, *Linn.. &c.*

This elegant shell may be distinguished from the varieties of *pereger*, which bear a close resemblance in many respects, by the exceedingly small acute spire, and capacious mouth, which occupies about two-thirds of the area. Is is of a shining horn colour, coarsely wrinkled, and more or less longitudinally striated; the outer lip is expanded and reflexed, forming a slight umbilical hollow behind. Length an inch, breadth three quarters of an inch.

var. ACUTUS, has the mouth less capacious and the body much smaller; spire very similar.

Animal of an olivaceous yellowish grey, with spots.

Hab. This shell is found chiefly in the southern and midland counties, and may be considered somewhat local, as it is wanting in many districts. Abundant in many places round London. The recorded localities are Clumber Lakes, Notts, York, Hemsworth dam near Ackworth, &c. It prefers still waters.

L. BURNETTI. *Alder.* Pl. VII, fig. 40.

Wrinkled, mouth very ample, folds indistinct; spire depressed, almost level.

Gulnaria lacustris, *Leach.*

This shell was first detected by Burnett, of Newcastle, in the stomach of trout caught in Lock Shene, Dumfriesshire, where it was taken alive. It is closely allied to some of the many varieties of *L. pereger*. The body whorl is large and broadly tumid in the middle, displaying a capacious sub-pyriform mouth. Length two-thirds of an inch, breadth one-half.

var. LACUSTRIS. Forbes and Hanley remark, (Hist. B. M., vol. IV, p. 175,) "With some hesitation we annex as a variety of this species, *Limnæus pereger, var.* 4, *(lacustris,)* of Gray's Manual. The apex is eroded, not quite sunken, and yet barely elevated above the body whorl, the pillar is much appressed. It is not improbable that this and the typical *Burnetti* may prove in the end to be the abnormal forms of *pereger.*"

Hab. Deep water, lakes, &c.

L. STAGNALIS. *Linnæus.* Pl. VII, fig. 34.

Shell conic, ovate; spire long, beautifully turreted and acute; whorls six or seven, the lower ones much inflated, displaying a capacious pyriform mouth.

Helix stagnalis, *Linn., &c.*

This most elegant *Limnæus* is often an inch and a half in length, and an inch in breadth; the shell is of a greyish white colour; the spire produced and conical, consisting of six whorls which are convex and turned, at times subangulated, separated by an oblique profound suture. The mouth is usually pyriform. Outer lip large in full grown specimens, and flattened in the middle. This shell varies much in size and thickness. It almost always presents a more or less lunated appearance.

var. FRAGILIS, much smaller and thinner, the body not so large and more regularly convex; spire longer in proportion, the whorls of which are more regularly convex and depressed, not lineated. It somewhat resembles the young of *stagnalis*, but is found separate and distinct. Animal olivaceous yellow, paler beneath.

Hab. Common in most parts of England, except the south west and some of the mountainous districts; the variety is somewhat more local and gregarious in its habits. We have found them abundantly in the south of Durham, and north of Yorkshire. Stagnant and slow waters.

L. TRUNCATULUS. *Muller*. Pl. VII, fig. 35.

Shell elongated, conic oval, perforated; spire long and consisting of six deeply divided volutions.

Helix fossaria, *Mont.* Limneus minutus, *Pfeif., &c.*

The smallest of the *Limnæi*, seldom attaining half-an-inch in length and three lines in breadth, of a pale horn colour, smooth and glossy. In shape it resembles *palustris*, but is much smaller and has the volutions rounder and more deeply and abruptly divided. They are extremely variable in size, according to the locality in which they are found. Animal of a light or dusky grey.

Hab. On the margin of muddy streams, in marshy places, &c., often covering itself with a coating of mud, probably for the twofold purpose of retaining the moisture and protecting it from observation. Generally diffused throughout the British Isles, and common in many places.

L. GLABER. *Muller*. Pl. VII, fig. 36.

Shell elongated, cylindrical, tapering; whorls rounded; aperture elongate, ovate, small.

Helix octanfracta, *Mont.* Limneus elongatus, *Drap.*

Shell longer than *truncatulus* and more gradually tapering, thin, glossy, and horn coloured, but often covered with a dark epidermis. Whorls seven or eight in number, and varying much in convexity; suture profund, slanting; body whorl not quite so long as the spire. About three quarters of an inch in length, by one quarter in breadth, but varies much in size. Animal blackish or dusky.

Hab. This shell is widely diffused, but rather local, and by no means abundant; it inhabits ponds or ditches of stagnant water, in Wilts, Somersetshire, Staffordshire, near Pontefract, York, and many parts of Yorkshire, Durham, and Northumberland; probably more common in the north than the south of England.

L. palustris. *Linnæus.* Pl. VII, fig. 39.

Shell ovate, oblong, spire tapering, of a purplish raw-umber colour; aperture ovate about the same length as the spire.

Helix palustris, *Gmel.*, *&c.*

This shell varies very much in size, shape, and colour, but cannot well be confused with any other species. It is generally an inch or more long and half-an-inch broad. Whorls seven, hardly raised, but divided by a distinct oblique suture. Aperture about half as long as the shell, of a chocolate colour inside; outer lip regularly arched. Animal dusky grey, tinged with olive.

Hab. Stagnant waters, with muddy bottoms, in most parts of the British Isles, and found more abundantly than the three preceding.

L. glutinosus. *Muller.* Pl. VII, fig. 32.

Shell subglobose, thin and transparent, finely wrinkled; of a pal amber colour, spire very small; aperture large.

Helix glutinosa, *Mont.* Amphipeplea glutinosa, *Gray.*

The shell of this species is extremely thin and highly polished. The spire is much depressed, consisting of three whorls ending obtusely; the body whorl is remarkably large, forming a capacious mouth, extending almost the whole length of the shell, which is ovate but acute above. About half-an-inch in length and three eighths in breadth. Animal large, of a pale dull yellow colour, with brighter spots; mantle lobes dilated; tentacles broad and flat.

Hab. This shell is rare, though at times rather plentiful where it occurs. The south eastern counties, the Cherwell, Oxfordshire, Lake Windermere, &c., are recorded localities. It seems to prefer deep and still waters.

L. involutus. *Harvey.* Pl, VII, fig. 33.

Shell ovate, thin, transparent; spire flat, consisting of three or four volutions; aperture large, pear shaped.

Amphipeplea involuta, *Gray*.

This rare *Limnæus* has only been discovered in one locality. It is thus described by the late W. Thompson, "Shell polished, extremely thin, of a pale amber colour, with coarse longitudinal striæ. It approaches *L. glutinosus* more nearly than any other species. The aperture is very large, wide at the base and extending to the apex; margin reflected only when it joins the pillar." About five lines in length and three and a half in breadth.

Hab. A small Alpine lake, at Cromaglaun mountain, near Killarney.

ANCYLUS. *Geoffroy*.

Shell—*Limpet shaped, conical ovate, simple and recurved; aperture ample, interrupted; apex on the left side by a semi-lunar scar; no operculum.*

Animal—*Conical, filling the whole of the shell, head broad, tentacles triangular; mantle simple, not reflected.*

A. FLUVIATILIS. *Muller*. Pl. VII, fig. 37.

Shell conoid; the apex recurved and near one end, bent to the right; aperture oval.

Patella lacustris, *Linn*.

The fresh water limpets, for so these shells are denominated, are very much like the marine *Patellæ*, and were for a long time placed by naturalists under that genus. The shell of *fluviatilis* is about a quarter of an inch in length, two lines and a half in breadth, and almost as high as long. It is semi-transparent, but covered with an olivaceous or black epidermis, slightly striated. The inside of the shell bluish white and glossy. Animal light grey.

Hab. Abundant on stones, in clear brooks or running streams, in all parts of the British Isles.

A. OBLONGUS. *Lightfoot*. Pl. VII, fig. 38.

Shell elongated, oblong, compressed; apex in the middle and very slightly recurved, bent to the left; aperture oblong.

Ancylus lacustris, *Mull.* Patella oblonga, *Light.* Velletia lacustris, *Gray.*

This little mollusk may be readily distinguished from the former species by being more elongated and depressed; having the apex less recurved, and to the left instead of the right; it is also thinner and more transparent. The apex is placed near the centre of the shell. Length a quarter of an inch; breadth the ninth of an inch. Animal dark grey, dextral, similar to *fluviatilis*, except in the dentition.

Hab. Generally distributed in England, but somewhat local, it prefers stagnant ponds, and is generally found adhering to grass and aquatic plants.

AURICULIDÆ.

CONOVOLUS. *Lamark.*

Shell—*Spiral, oval; aperture ovate, pyriform, entire, toothed within; outer lip simple or slightly reflected, more or less thickened. No operculum.*

Animal—*With two triangular and ringed tentacles, having eyes at their inner bases.*

C. BIDENTATUS. *Montagu.* Pl. VII, fig. 43.

Shell ovate, ventricose, smooth; pillar with two folds.

Voluta bidentata, *Mont.*

The shells belonging to this species vary in shape, but are uniformly of a yellowish horn colour above and white underneath the periostraca. Whorls six or seven, small and moderately convex. It has two teeth or folds on the inner lip, as the name implies, which readily distinguish it from any other of the genus. The spire of the shell is sometimes eroded. Not quite a quarter of an inch in length, breadth a line and a half.

var. ALBUS, (Pl. VII. fig. 44,) narrower, slenderer, and more fragile; spire more produced.

Animal white, with two very flat, short, setose tentaculæ, with eyes at their inner bases.

Hab. The *conovuli* inhabit brackish water near the sea, in crevices of rocks near high water mark. The recorded localities are Devon and Cornwall, and other places on the south-west coast, Isle of Man, near Middlesbro', &c.

C. DENTICULATUS. *Montagu.* Pl. VII, fig. 42.

Shell oblong, smooth, coloured, spire conical; aperture pyriform, protected by more than two teeth.

Voluta denticulata, *Mont.*

The individuals included under this species vary much in size, in colour, and in the length of the spire and convexity of the whorls. The mouth contains three or six teeth, which are sometimes distinct, at others nearly obsolete, they are placed on both sides the aperture. It differs from *bidentatus* in the colour of the shell, (which is a purplish brown above a yellowish horn coloured periostraca,) and in the position of the teeth. Length about a third of an inch, breadth two lines. The variety *myosotis* is similar except in the aperture, but for the most part stronger and of a deeper tint of colouring. Inner lip with only two or three teeth, outer lip with one. Animal yellowish or bluish white, tentacles filiform and compressed, with eyes at their inner bases.

Hab. Brackish water in the neighbourhood of the sea. More common in the south than in the north of England. We have however met with it at Middlesbro'. The variety occurs in the Thames and Avon, near Bristol, as well as other places.

CARYCHIUM. *Muller.*

Shell—*Spiral, thin, cylindrical, aperture small, oblong, toothed; peristome thickened; no operculum.*

Animal—*With an elongated ringed muzzle, two cylindrical obtuse tentacles, with eyes at their inner bases.*

C. MINIMUM. *Muller.* Pl. VII, fig. 46.

Turbo carychium, *Gruel.* Auricula minima, *Drap.*, *&c.*

This smallest of British shells may be readily distinguished by its pretty little white or cream coloured, tapering, cylindrical, and spiral shell, which is a line in length and half a line in breadth. Whorls five or six in number, moderately rounded, end tapering to a blunt apex; peristome broadly reflected. The aperture suboval, provided with three or four teeth, one on the outer lip, two on the inner, and one on the pillar lip.

var. SUBEDENTULUM, with the teeth almost obsolete.

Animal creamy white with large eyes.

Hab. Generally diffused over the British Isles. It may be found by carefully looking amongst moss, grass, &c., in damp situations.

CYCLOSTOMIDÆ.

CYCLOSTOMA. *Montfort.*

Shell—*Ovate, spiral, turreted, mouth simple, oval; with an operculum consisting of four or five oval depressed whorls, terminating in an excentric nucleus.*

Animal—*With a proboscidiform muzzle; two subulate tentacles, with eyes at their external bases.*

C. ELEGANS. *Muller.* Pl. VII, fig. 48.

This is the only British representative of this interesting genus of mollusks. It may be readily distinguished by its thick strong shell, which is covered by a purplish brown periostraca which is marked with numerous, close-set, raised, longitudinal striæ. Whorls five, simply rounded; sutures profound and rather oblique; spire turreted, and terminating in a blunt apex, much sculptured; mouth circular, inside of a reddish colour. The shell is dextral; length half an inch, breadth one third of an inch.

The variety *marmorea* of Brown, is much smaller and more finely striated.

Animal of a dark brown colour, with an elongated head and subulated tentacles.

Hab. Hedges, under stones, &c., in chalk and limestone districts. It occurs at Hemsley, Thorpe, Hackfall near Ripon, and other places in Yorkshire, near Kendal, and most parts of the south of England.

ACME. *Hartman.*

Shell—*Cylindrical, spiral, turreted, obtuse at the apex; aperture ovate, entirely toothless; operculum very thin and corneous.*

Animal—*With two long and slender tentacles, with eyes at their inner bases.*

A. LINEATA. *Draparnaud.* Pl. VII, fig. 47.

This delicate little gem, which is by no means common, may be readily distinguished from *C. minimum,* which it nearly resembles in size, by being more cylindrical and having a blunter apex, and being of a brownish or rufous colour. Whorls six, slightly raised but well defined. Mouth small and circular. Length of the shell about one-tenth of an inch, and about half that in breadth. Animal much the same colour as the shell.

Hab. Rare and local in England and Ireland, not found in Scotland. It has been found in Northumberland; Airyholme Wood, Hemsley, and Ripon, in Yorkshire; Oxfordshire; and one or two other places. It prefers very damp situations, at the roots of moss and Hepatica, in woods containing peaty soil.

GLOSSARY OF CONCHOLOGICAL TERMS.

Anterior. In bivalves is the side on which the head, or part analagous to the head of the animal lies.

Aperture or Mouth. The entrance to the spiral cavity of univalve shells.

Apex. The top or nucleus of the shell, from which point the shell, enlarging as it descends, takes a spiral, arched, straight, oblique, or irregular course.

Axis. The imaginary line, round which the whorls of a spiral shell revolve.

Bivalve. A shell composed of two separate pieces.

Body Whorl. The last whorl, constituting the bulk of the shell.

Byssus. The fibres by which some bivalve shells adhere to stones, &c., under the water.

Cardinal Teeth. The teeth upon the hinge directly beneath the umbones of a bivalve shell, as distinguished from the *lateral* teeth, which are placed at a distance on each side.

Carinated. Applied to any shell having a raised, thin edge.

Cinereous. Ash-coloured.

Clausium. A ligamentous membrane attached to the animal of Clausilia. (See genus Clausilia, p. 52.)

Clavate. When one extremity of the shell is attenuated, and the other becomes suddenly rounded.

Columella. A solid column found by the inner sides of the volutions of spiral univalves.

Columella lip. The inner lip.

Concentric. A term applied to the direction taken by the lines of growth in spiral and other shells, (*longitudinal* of some authors).

Corneous. Horny.

Corroded. When the umbones, apices, and other parts of shells are worn away by water.

Crenated. Applied to small notches not sufficiently defined to be called teeth.

Decussate. Intersected by striæ crossing each other.

Denticulated. Having little teeth or raised points.

Dextral. Place the point of a spiral shell towards the eye with the mouth downwards; if the aperture be on the right side of the axis, it is a *dextral* shell, if otherwise, it is *sinistral* or reversed.

Discoidal. When the whorls form a flattened spire.

Dorsal. A dorsal shell is one placed upon the back of the animal. The dorsal margin of a bivalve shell is that on which the hinge is placed; the opposite is called *ventral.*

Epidermis. The fibrous, horny, external coating of shells. The outer covering of extraneous matter with which some shells are generally coated.

Epiphragm. The membranous or calcareous substance with which some mollusks close the aperture, when they retire to hibernate.

Equivalve. A term applied to a bivalve shell when the valves are equal to each other in dimensions.

External. A shell which contains the animal, and is not covered by the mantle.

Granulated. Covered with minute rough grains.

Hinge. The edge of the bivalve shells near the umbones, including the teeth and ligament.

Inequilateral. A term applied to a bivalve shell when its extent on one side of the umbones is greater than that on the other.

Inequivalve. The two principal valves differing from each other in diameter or convexity.

Inflected or Inflexed. Turned inwards. Applied to the lip of a spiral shell when turned towards the body whorl.

Inner lip. That edge of the aperture of a univalve shell, which is near to the imaginary axis, as distinguished from the *outer* lip, or that which is on the outer side.

Internal ligament. The ligament of a bivalve shell which is placed within the closed part of the hinge, so as not to be seen when the valve is shut.

Keel. A flattened ridge, resembling the keel of a ship.

Lamellated. Having the layers of which the shell is composed overlaying each other.

Lateral. The lateral teeth take their rise near the umbones, and proceed towards the sides of the shell.

Ligament. The external substance by which the two valves of bivalve shells are connected.

Lip. The inner lip, or *labium*, is used to express that side of the aperture nearest to the axis; the outer lip, or *labrum*, is the edge of the aperture at the greatest distance from the axis.

Longitudinal. Lengthwise. Longitudinal striæ, &c.

Mantle. The cutaneous and fleshy envelope which invests the interior of the shell of *conchifera;* in Limaces the external fleshy substance covering the shell, sometimes called the *shield.*

Marginated. Having an edge or border thicker than the rest.

Nucleus. A kernel. Anything forming a centre round which matter is gathered. The nucleus of a shell is the first part formed; generally applied to the apex of spiral shells.

Oblique. In a slanting direction. The whorls of spiral univalves generally take an oblique direction, in reference to the imaginary axis of the shell.

Obsolete. Used to express an indistinctness of character.

Obtuse. Blunt; generally used to express the character ot the spire.

Operculum. The plate which serves to protect the aperture in some mollusks.

Patelliform. Shaped like a disk.

Pedicle or Peduncle. The stem or organ of attachment of some water-shells

Pellucid. Clear and somewhat transparent.

Periostraca. The natural epidermis or thin skin which covers some shells.

Peristome. The lip or rim that surrounds the aperture of most univalves.

Pillar. The name of the column which forms the axis of spiral shells, round which the whole revolves.

Plait or Fold. A term generally applied to the prominences on the inner lip of some univalve shells.

Posterior. The posterior, or hinder part of a bivalve shell, is that in which the siphonal tube of the animal is placed.

Pyriform. Shaped like a pear, that is large and rounding at one end and gradually tapering at the other.

Radiating. A term applied to the ribs, striæ, bands of colour, &c., when they meet in a point at the umbones of a bivalve shell.

Reflected or reflexed. Turned or folded backwards.

Reversed or Sinistral. See *Dextral.*

Septa. The internal laminar division between the whorls of most univalve shells.

Simple. Single, entire, uninterrupted, undivided.

Sinistral. On the left side, reversed.

Spines. Thin pointed spikes.

Spiral. Revolving from a centre.

Spire. The cone or pyramid of some univalve shells. The spire, in descriptions, includes all the whorls above the mouth of the shell.

Striæ, striulæ. Small channels in shells.

Sulcated. Having grooves or furrows.

Suture. A seam, stitch, or joining together; applied particularly to the line which marks the joining of the whorls of the spire.

Tentacle. A filiform process round the mouth of various mollusks, being either an organ of feeling, prehension, or motion.

Transverse. Crosswise.

Turreted. When the whorls of univalve shells rise regularly above each other, so as to have the appearance of little turrets.

Umbilicus. The hollow in a spiral shell, occasioned by its whorls or convolutions not touching each other.

Umbones. The points in bivalve shells which constitute the nucleus or apex of each valve, and are generally situated near the hinge.

Univalve, consisting of only one shell or valve.

Ventral. The margin of a bivalve shell, opposite the hinge.

Ventricose. Rounded out.

Whorl or Volution. A wreath, convolution, or turn of the spire of a univalve shell.

INDEX.

A FEW REMARKS

ON THE

COLLECTING OF SHELLS,

FOR OUR YOUNGER READERS.

ALTHOUGH the descriptions and observations under each species, would, perhaps, be sufficient to enable the Conchologist readily to discover and name them; we have thought a few remarks, addressed more especially to our younger readers, in a simple manner, might be of use in conveying some hints of a practical character, which could not be so well introduced in any other way. We will, therefore, take an imaginary conchological trip.

What a merry company we are, on this our first hunt after shells. "I wonder how many we shall find?" says one; "I can't imagine what they are like," replies his companion, "unless they are those striped snails which we find in the hedge banks; but here comes Cousin William, who will tell us all about them;" whereupon, with many a pleasant joke and merry laugh, we make our way to the nearest stream, dash in our spoons with impatient ardour, and having brought up a quantity of mud from the bottom, look into the slimy mass in despair. Oh! Cousin William, how could you bring us to such a spot as this; who can find any shells among this filthy stuff? "Patience, my dear boy, shake it about well in the water to clear off the mud, and you will most likely find what you want left behind; next time, however, you apply your spoon, put it in a little more gently, and scrape off the top of the mud only, or run it through the plants in the middle of the stream, or amongst the grass on the margin, and you will obtain that for which you are searching, without all the labour you are now giving yourself." Having followed out our instructions, after a deal of labour by our unskilful hands, we soon perceive some light coloured objects, which, upon close inspection, turn out to be shells. "Oh! what lovely little things," we all exclaim in a breath, "see, they are double shells!"

Being now fairly in quest of these inhabitants of the stream, we quickly fill some of our boxes with the bivalves, and with one or two kinds of univalves. The first excitement is after a while somewhat over, and we sit down upon some grassy knoll to look over our spoils. Cousin William is applied to for information respecting them; he explains to his young companions that the bivalves first found belong to the order *Conchifera;* that they are called *Cyclas Cornea;* that there are three species included under the head *Cyclas,* and a variety of other information respecting them. He next shews them some of the other smaller bivalves, allied to the *Cyclas*, but under another family, named *Pisidium*—the one they have found being *Pisidium amnicum.* "Whatever is this!" exclaims a youthful member of our party, "see what a slimy looking animal protrudes himself from the large opening!" This turns out to be *Limnæus pereger*, the most widely distributed of our water shells, and though by no means the most attractive-looking object, it improves on acquaintance. "You have overlooked this pretty little shining fellow," remarks their interesting instructor, "it is the 'bubble shell,' *Physa fontinalis*—take care, or you will break it, it is too fragile to be roughly handled." Some other curious looking shells are next brought under review; they are all flat, and consist of five or six whorls close together, very much like a minute snake when coiled up; these, they are informed, belong to the genus *Planorbis*, the larger one being *marginatus*, and the smaller and thinner ones, *vortex*.

On our next trip, though the novelty is not so great as before, we set out with redoubled zeal, puffed up with the consciousness of having no small acquaintance with what we are about. Our first dip affords us some of our former acquaintances, but nothing new rewards our search; so we pass on to a small pond, which has been espied by one of our party, in the corner of a large field. "Did you ever see such a huge fellow!" calls out one of our juvenile band, throwing down his spoon, and rushing with outstretched hands to Cousin William, who seems no less pleased than his young friend, to meet with what he informs him belongs to the same family as *Limnœus pereger*, giving it the name of *Limnæus stagnalis*. It does not require very minute search to observe quite a number of them floating about with their broad expanded foot upward on the surface of the water, nor does it take long to obtain a sufficient supply. Whilst examining our prizes more carefully, and admiring their beautiful tapering forms, we find adhering closely to their surface, a small oblong limpet-like shell, which Cousin William calls *Ancylus oblongus*, and informs us that a commoner species, *Ancylus fluviatilis*, may be generally found in clear running streams adhering to stones, wood, &c.

One earnest member of our company expecting, or

wishing, to find nearly all the different species within the narrow limits of a single pond, exclaims with a rather disappointed air, "I have searched and searched, but cannot find a single *Limnæus pereger.*" This, he is told, is by no means an uncommon thing, though the reason is less easily given; he is also informed, that frequently in the same stream, in one part nearly all shells are of a species differing from those inhabiting another. At the bottom of one slowly flowing stream, several large bivalves are pointed out to us, sunk almost over-head in mud; these turn out to be ***Anodonta Cygnea.*** With no little eagerness we apply our spoons, but without much effect, except upon those which are tenantless; looking to our preceptor, who is smiling at our attempts, we entreat him to help us, but he shakes his head, and says we must move on to a part of the stream which is clearer than that we have disturbed. Here we watch him quietly plunge the handle of his spoon into the water, and insert it between the valves of one of these shells, and draw it out again with it firmly attached to the end.

Our next Conchological excursion, we are informed, is to be confined more particularly to those which inhabit woods, and hedge-rows; and we set out without any definite idea as to what we are likely to meet with. The first convenient mossy bank is, however, submitted to a search; down we drop on our knees, pull aside the leaves and stems of the plants, and after diligent search, we find several species, chiefly of the ***Helix*** and ***Zonites*** tribe; ***Pupa umbilicata*** and also ***Bulimus obscurus*** are added to our stock, though but sparingly. Thence we proceed to a wood of more ancient growth, where the soil, for some depth, is little else than a carbonaceous deposit of decayed vegetable matter ; here, so numerous are the different species, that we have neither time nor ability to make any classification of them, so depositing them in some of our boxes, having more regard to their size than specific distinctions, being afraid if we mix the smaller with the larger, that they may be lost or injured.

Following the guidance of our leader, we traverse the wood in all directions; now examining the roots of plants; now carefully scanning the stems and leaves of the dense masses of ferns, Equisetæ, and the larger herbaceous plants, with which the place is crowded, for the more conspicuous of the *Helices* and *Succinea putris*. Nor do we forget to pry in the bark, and beneath the Lichens which clothe the stems of the huge oaks around us, being assured that we shall most probably be rewarded with some of the *Clausilia* tribe, or, perhaps, *Balea fragilis*. Coming to an old stump, we are advised to examine it well, as it will most likely afford us some interesting specimens, and sure enough, we have not been long busily engaged amongst the moss which clothes its decayed sides, before one of our party exclaims exultingly, " I have it, I have it ! " and exhibits to our eager and enquiring gaze the most elegant land shell we have yet found, *Clausilia laminata*, and we seem as though we could scarcely cease admiring its deep pellucid chocolate colour, the gracefulness of its swelling outline, and the curious wavy tooth which protects its mouth. Several others are found, and we wend our way homewards.

Living within a few miles of the sea coast, and understanding there are a number of Land Shells to be found upon the sand-hills in the neighbourhood of the sea, it is not long before we determine upon an excursion thither. Accordingly, one fine day, we might be seen exploring most earnestly what might seem to many persons the most uninteresting locality imaginable; we, however, do not find it so, for we are quite surprised at the immense number of *Helix virgata*, *ericetorum*, *Cantiana*, and *caperata*, which find their subsistence upon the low stunted vegetation. In one part, too, we come upon a numerous family of *Pupa muscorum*, and at other places meet with *Helix hispida*, variety *depilata*, and have some of our notions of specific difference rather shaken, by being told that it is not a distinct species.

A piece of marshy ground in the neighbourhood is next explored; there we find the first specimens of *Conovulus* we have seen, which, though placed among the Land Shells, or rather, perhaps, the amphibious ones, seems to prefer situations where the water is slightly brackish. Proceeding onwards in our search, we come to the margin of a considerable stream, on whose banks there is a quantity of rejectmenta, or "wreck," as it is sometimes called, which has been brought down by a flood; this, when examined, proves to be rich in the empty homes of several species of mollusks, some of which we have not seen before. A portion is taken home, to be examined at leisure. Thus an excursion which might have seemed at first likely to afford little that would interest one in the search of Land shells merely, turns out to be more than usually productive, and many leisure hours are employed, in cleaning, naming, and arranging those which we have thus procured.

Many are the instructive lessons we receive respecting the habits and economy of the different tribes; their internal structure is also a subject of a good deal of interest. The stomach of one of the larger ones is exhibited to our wondering eyes, and shown, under the microscope, to be lined by a thin gizzard-like membrane, armed with some thousands of horny teeth, for the purpose of masticating the food; the stomach being set in motion by a large muscle.

The pulsation of the heart of these creatures is watched with great interest, and one or two instructive experiments are made upon them. A large specimen of *Limax cinereus* is first obtained, and being placed on a plate, or some shallow vessel, is allowed free liberty of action; this he presently takes advantage of, and stretching himself to his full length, begins his peregrinations; almost simultaneously with this we perceive his breathing hole expand, displaying all the internal structure of that part of the body just beneath the mantle; the lungs and the heart are easily discernible. Wishing for a closer inspection of these, we apply our magnifying glasses, and thus perceive a sight which astonishes us. The whole arrangement of the heart, with its network of arteries and veins, is rendered quite distinct, and by careful observation, we can discern the repeated filling and emptying of these, as the muscles of the heart expand or contract; counting the strokes we find that *Limax cinereus* has a pulsation of 60 or 70 strokes per minute, and this we find to be the ordinary rate of most other land mollusks, under a temperature of about 60° Fahrenheit.

We next place under review several different species of the most transparent *Zonites*, examining them with a pocket lens. The heart is best seen when the shell is placed with the under surface upwards; the pulsation is very distinctly discernible, though the arteries can scarcely be seen on account of the thickness of the shell intervening. The number of strokes is as above mentioned when the shell is placed on the table, but we no sooner take it into our hands, than its pulsation is increased to an almost feverish rapidity, and we count upward of 100 strokes per minute. This seems really marvellous, and we immediately exclaim, " What can be the cause of this? it cannot arise from fear, it surely must be the heat of the hand;" so, in order to test the the truth of this surmise, we prepare a cooling mixture, and place our subject so that it may be affected by the cold without being wetted. Our theory is verified, for in a very few seconds their pulsations seem almost to cease, or to go on so languidly as to make it difficult to count the strokes; probably they may not be more than 20 per minute. But we soon perceive the benefit that is to result from such a provision; it is one of the many evidences of design on the part of an all-wise Creator, with which the animal kingdom abounds. During the winter, mollusks hybernate, and remain for several months in a state of torpor, without partaking of any nourishment, as is evident, since they seal up the entrance of their domain at the commencement of severe weather, and do not come forth until the warmth of spring calls them into more active existence.

How important, then, that as little waste as possible should go on during that period; and in no other way could this be brought about so effectually as in having the circulation decreased to such a degree as almost to cease during the severity of the winter season.

Pl. I.

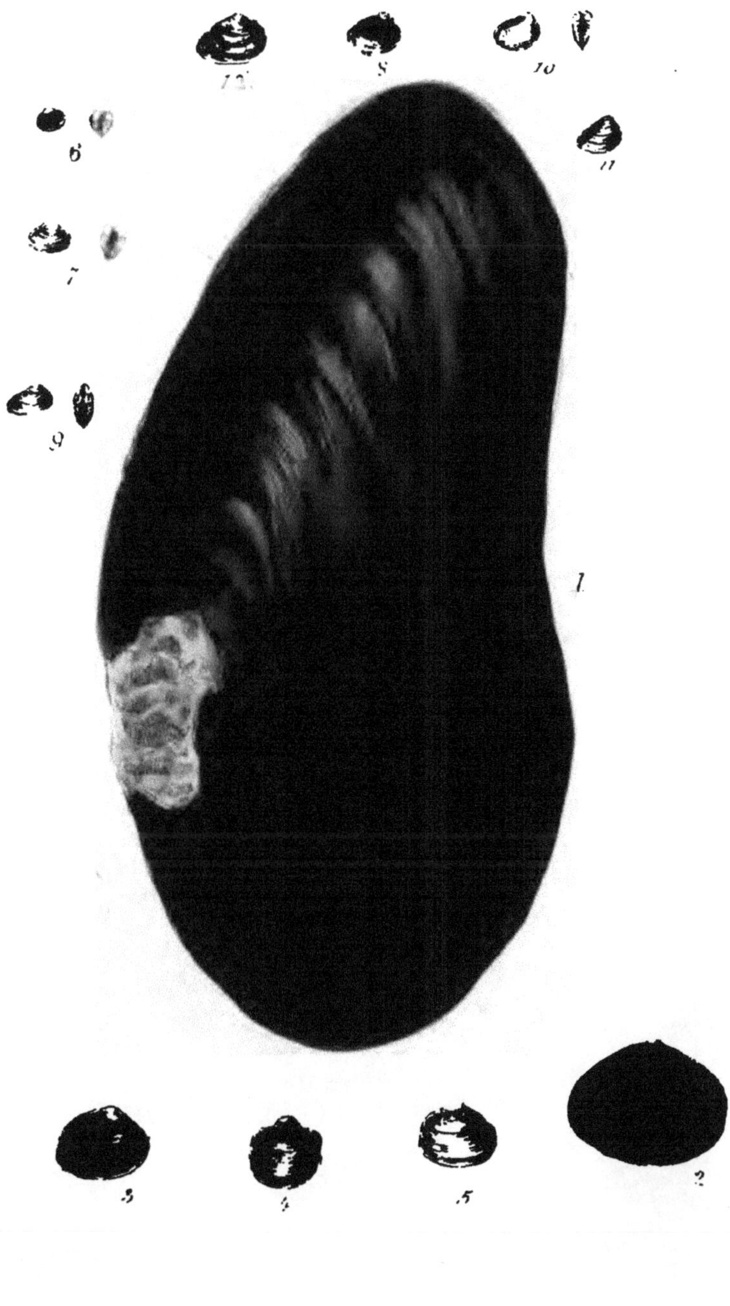

1.

Pl. III.

1

2

2×

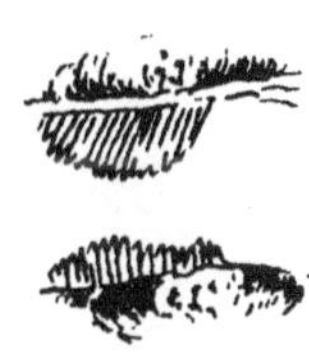

1×

3.

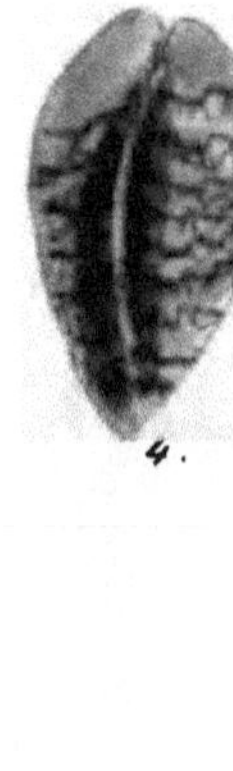

4.

Pl. IV

Pl. V.

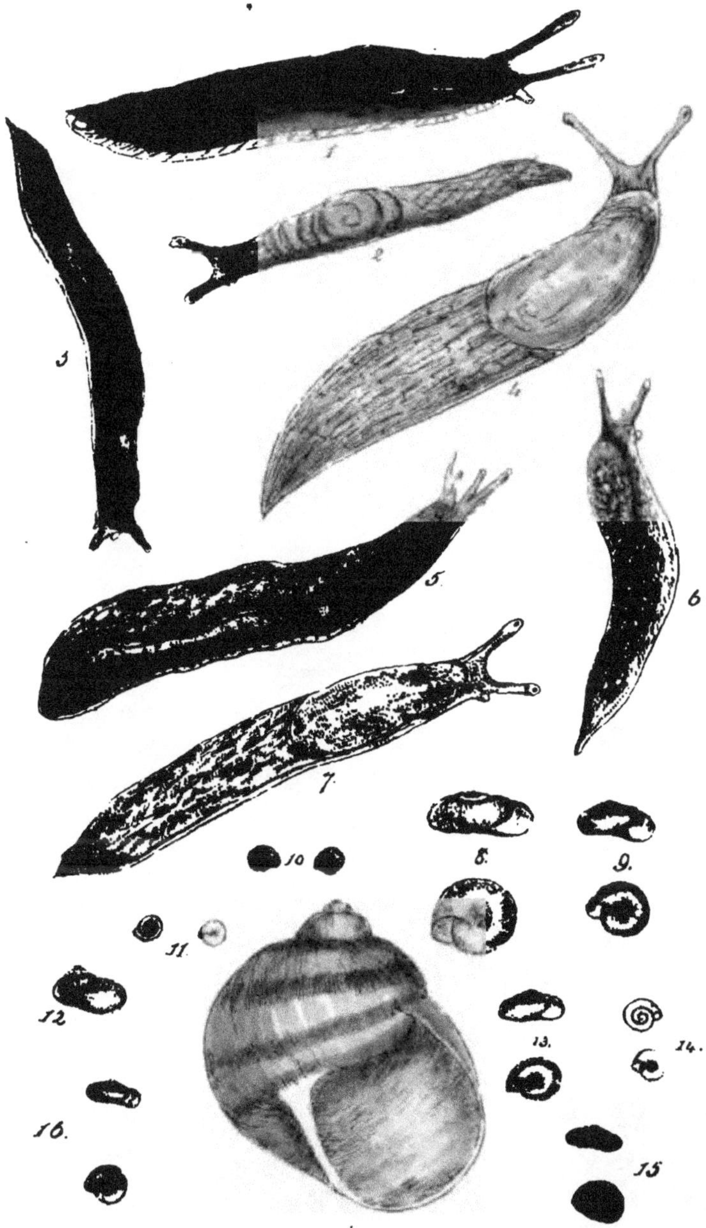

Pl. VI.

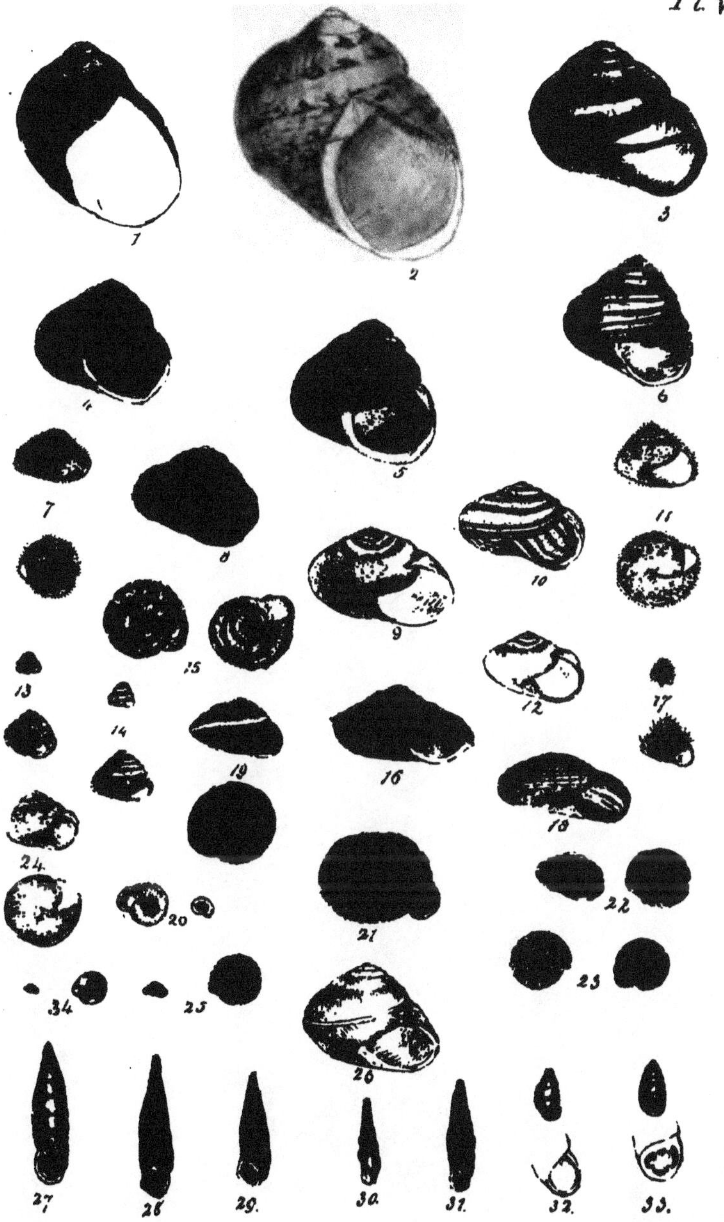
1
2
3
4
5
6
7
8
9
10
11
12
13
14
15
16
17
18
19
20
21
22
23
24
25
26
27
28
29.
30.
31.
32.
33.
34
25

Pl. VII.

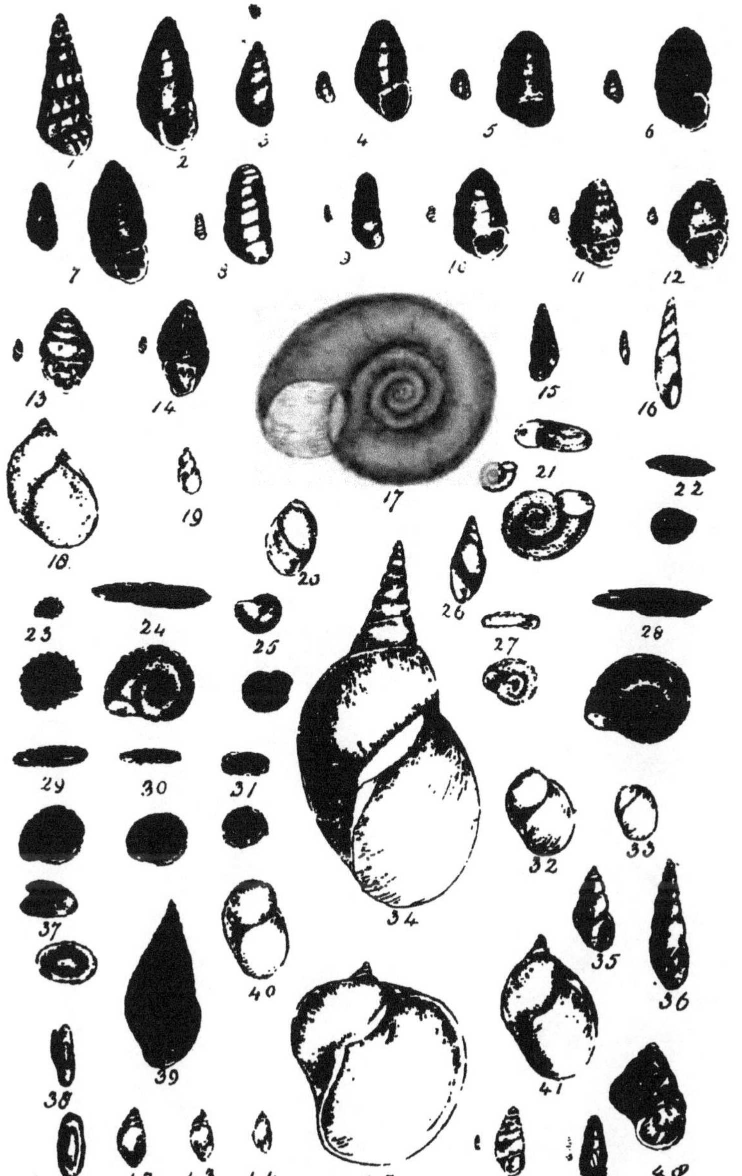
1
2
3
4
5
6
7
8
9
10
11
12
13
14
15
16
17
18
19
20
21
22
23
24
25
26
27
28
29
30
31
32
33
34
35
36
37
38
39
40
41
42
43
44
45
46
47
48

CPSIA information can be obtained
at www.ICGtesting.com
Printed in the USA
LVHW101952050123
736480LV00003B/300